The Dream of Althazar

To Gail –
Wise Counselor,
Bold Adventurer,
Enthusiastic Cheerleader,
but best of all
my dear, dear Friend!
May your Swash never Buckle!
Nancy Lee Young
Christmas 2006

The Dream of Althazar

A Novel

Nancy Lee Young

iUniverse, Inc.
New York Lincoln Shanghai

The Dream of Althazar

iUniverse books may be ordered through booksellers or by contacting:

iUniverse
2021 Pine Lake Road, Suite 100
Lincoln, NE 68512
www.iuniverse.com
1-800-Authors (1-800-288-4677)

ISBN-13: 978-0-595-41334-8 (pbk)
ISBN-13: 978-0-595-85687-9 (ebk)
ISBN-10: 0-595-41334-X (pbk)
ISBN-10: 0-595-85687-X (ebk)

Printed in the United States of America

Prologue

Once upon a time, long, long ages ago
the Earth was filled with wonderful, diverse Creatures
who dwelt in a Climate of Peace,
all speaking and understanding
one another in a common tongue.

There was civility and respect
and enough joy and goodness to go around,
so that all of God's Creation
could grow and prosper without conflict.

But, of course that was only a Dream.

However, the Dream would re-emerge from time to time,
And some Special Messenger would tell it again
to whomever would listen.

And they who heard,
and took the time to hear with their hearts,
would nod wisely (albeit with some sadness)
and say:

Yes, that is the way it was,
and probably should be—
and maybe will be, again, someday...

But, of course, that is only a Dream.

Book I

The Dream of Althazar

CHAPTER 1

INTRODUCTION TO THE DREAM

One very calm and clear night in early autumn, my father asked me to walk out with him. As his presence was one of my greatest pleasures, I eagerly joined in. The stars, that night, were so bright that they seemed to stitch earth to heaven with long strands of cold fire.

A large, familiar, dark, shape loomed up before me, and my mother rushed eagerly to join us. Her dear embrace was particularly long and loving. A deep rumble, almost a sob, shook her—and me—not our ordinary hug of greeting.

This unusual meeting of the three of us made me uneasy. I sensed a certain gravity in the walk that we were sharing. A feeling of anxiety of the unknown rushed through me.

We came to the edge of a meadow, and we stopped. In the luminous glow of the stars, everything was particularly bright, and I could see my parents in every loved detail.

My father enfolded me in his huge hug. Again, I heard and felt that rumbling of a great sob deep within. In alarm I pulled away, a prickle of fear raising the ruff on the back of my neck. My father read me at once:

"Do not be afraid, my son…no harm will ever come to you." My father's strong, confident voice reached out to comfort me:

"You are a King's son; you are ever in my protection—and the Star's. Tonight it has come to us—to you. Tonight you begin your life's journey."

He pointed upwards, and I saw the brightest and biggest star that I had ever seen. I had not noticed it until now, and that seemed very strange because it outshone every other star in the sky—a sky brilliant with bright stars!

My father continued. "That is your Guide and Guardian Star. It will watch over you and lead you on your Journey to your destiny. Neither your mother nor I know what or where that destination is. But, you have been entrusted to us to bring you to the beginning of this, your Journey. You have received all our knowledge and wisdom and skills as your inheritance. We cannot go any farther. You must go on alone, on your own, with your Star."

I was speechless—and shaking with shock and anxiety.

Then, my mother spoke:

"My dearest son, your education has included more than skills and necessities of a bear's everyday life. We have tried to lead you into the world of thought and ideas. The Journey-of-the-Star will probably take you farther into your mind than into the far reaches of our earth. But, you will find opportunities to explore both levels of experience. And, you will seek and find great wisdom on both levels.

"Oh dear. I sense your puzzlement and confusion. I know you hardly understand any of our serious, heavy words right now. Your father and I barely comprehend these ideas ourselves; but we believe that we have been led to share what we know. We believe—we trust—that you also will be led to wisdom deeper than ours, and a way to share it, in your Journey-of-the-Star.

"There will be dangers and hardships and great mysteries—but you will be ever in the protection of your Star." She reached out, touched my breast, and pointed to the star above us. I realized then that she was making a connection with the blazing overhead star and the white star that I had been born with, right over my heart.

I had never given much thought to my birthmark—many bears are born with white marks on their fur fronts. These mainly disappear with maturity. Mine, however, had endured. It was a four-pointed white star; its lower point longer than the other three, resting almost over my heart.

I had been teased about it in my cub-hood, and I was often called "Star Bear." But I had not paid much attention to its seeming permanence. (After all, it is not easy to get a glimpse in total—or perspective—of something that resides in the shadow of a large bear head and a long nose.)

My father moved over in front of me and raised something over my head, which he hung around my neck. He took my paw and wrapped it around the object that hung down over my birthmark. The object hung from a thick cord or thong, and it was warm, heavy, and smooth. It had four corners, with even points—and a hole in its center which tied it to its lanyard.

It felt wonderfully comforting to me, especially in my present state of anxiety. Right then, I just wanted to hold onto something.

My father said, "This is a very real connection with your lodestar. This is star stuff—an actual piece of a meteor, a meteorite.

"On the night of your birth, a piece of a shooting star fell through the sky into this very meadow, sizzling its way through trees and grasses to plow a deep black furrow into the earth.

"Your brothers and I ran to the field to see it and to stomp out any fires that the star might have left in its blazing entry into our kingdom. Lucky for us, the forests and fields were very wet, and there were no fires.

"We kept watch for days until our star cooled, and we could dig it out of its charred hole. This was—is—it, in its star shape, a piece of iron from that great universe over our heads—a piece of the great cosmos, not from our earth.

"Of course, I have kept it and treasured it. When you emerged from your birthing den, in your little fur suit, I was astonished to see that white star birthmark on your breast. I told your mother about the piece of iron from the sky. It was truly awesome!

"We both knew then that all this was a sign that you were to be a very different and special bear. We raised you accordingly. We have no idea what the Divine Source has in its plans for you. We only know that we have filled you with love and strength and wisdom, and your Journey, now, is out of our charge. And it is, most probably, a journey that will last your lifetime."

I stood speechless. My thoughts were racing and my heart was pounding. I felt a great welling up of tears. This was going to be the last time that I was to see my beloved father and mother. They were sending me out into the great unknown. Son of a King or not, I was terrified! Even a Prince might cry!

My parents waited quietly and patiently for my sobs to subside, at what a cost to them, I could not know.

Finally, my father spoke again. "Your Star looks to be leading you to the south. Follow it at night when it is clear and true. The iron Star-Stone will work to confirm your headings at other times, if so needed. Balance it from its center hole on a vertical twig; the notched corner will always point north—that is the magic of the magnetic iron Star-Stone. Trust in the Star and the Stone. Trust your heart, your intuition, and your instincts to be on your true course.

"You will travel through many strange and exotic lands, and you will meet many strange and exotic creatures along the way, but, as you know, we bears can speak in a language common to all creatures, so befriend all whom you meet—seek their counsel and wisdom. Treat all with compassion and courtesy. Share respect, treasure diversity in all creatures—seek Truth, seek Wisdom, seek Goodness—but, above all, be a Bearer of Peace!

"You are our beloved son—and no harm will ever come to you. Behold your Star. Begin your Journey. Your mother and I love you more than life."

Then each in turn hugged me long and strong and turned to silently melt into the forest and the night.

Chapter 2

Expectations

I was born a long, long time ago, the last son of the wise and powerful King Althar. My name is Althazar.

My father was very old at the time of my birth, and all his earlier sons and daughters had gone off to build their own families and territories within our vast kingdom of the Northern Forests.

As the newest and youngest son, with others ahead of me in the line of succession, there was no thought of my ever becoming King. So my status was royal and privileged, but with no great responsibilities or future kingly expectations. Or, so I thought.

Our kingdom was in a heavily forested, mountainous part of what, at that time, was a vast wild continent.

I was a species of Great Brown Bears (although I was a dark, dark brown, almost black in color). Where we reigned, we were acknowledged as being on the top of the power structure. Our family ruled and roamed over large areas of wild lands where food and shelter were rich and abundant.

There were many other creatures in the forests and meadows, but life was structured then so that we seldom clashed.

Life was easy and uncomplicated for me—all I had to do was grow and learn and enjoy all the advantages of my youthful privileges (and energies). My mother taught me all her earth skills and watched patiently over my life lessons, as boisterous and silly as I often made them.

(Bear cubs take a little longer to mature than some other creatures; they have so much to learn. Curiosity and intelligence, driven by natural playfulness and energy, demanded a lot of parental supervision.) I was fortunate to have almost the full attention of both my mother and father. Unusual, as most bear fathers do not stay around for the nurturing process. Bears, by nature, are mostly loners; my mother and father were not typical of our species. As it turned out, neither was I!

I remember one day especially, a true turning-point day, when my mother decided that I was ready to graduate from the pranks and play of cub-hood to the serious business of adult bear-hood. It was the only time she ever swatted me for real; and, looking back on the occasion, I deserved it.

We were out foraging for food. My mother was trying to train me on obvious food sources, like buzzing bees that led us to honey—and less obvious sources like underneath vibrations. I was trying to pay attention, but my hunger had not been fully appeased (and mother was no longer a willingly available milk source). We were in a deadfall area. Many fallen trees were rotting on the ground around us and under these trees many living insects and grubs were at work, just ready for becoming lunch for hungry bears.

My mother turned over several very ripe logs and the two of us feasted readily, although these feasts were more appetizers than a fulsome meal.

The morning progressed from log to log. Mother spotted and overturned each log. We snacked. The time came when she sat down and told me to do likewise.

She said: "What are you thinking?"

"Lunch," I replied without hesitation.

"Well that's a start…I want you to become a thinking bear as well as a doer. You do understand what it is to think, don't you?" (I thought I did, think, that is.)

Mother continued, "What are you thinking now?"

"Lunch," I replied again.

She blew out her cheeks in an exasperated whiffle, and tried once more. "Now, when you think of lunch, I presume you have some sort of image in mind—grubs, honey, berries, and acorns. Hopefully, you see yourself going after those foods in some practical way. You have a goal—lunch—and you have a means, a way to achieve that goal. Am I right?"

"Lunch," I repeated, stubbornly, not really willing to play a game of words when food was in sight, not *in mind.*

I got up to go to another rotten log. That is when my mother swatted me. I rolled over and over, caught off-guard, not realizing how far I had overplayed that stubborn mind-set.

"*Now*, do I have your full attention?" She wasn't particularly angry; she was determined.

I decided that lunch was not quite as important, at that moment, as was my mother's approval. She was a lot bigger and wiser, and she had the paw-power!

I crept back to her side in a posture of submission and respect. The paw that met me was one of tenderness and forgiveness this time. She patted me on the head and continued her instructions. (She had my full attention!)

"You are a Special Bear, Althazar," she said, "you must learn to think, to use your imagination, to ask (in your mind) *what if*...and to work out questions and answers in your mind. These mental forays are called Ideas, and you will learn to search and find and work out Ideas as effectively as you search for lunch!

"Now, there is a rotten log, what plan do you have in mind to attain your goal of lunch—that is, what have you learned from watching me and recalling your own experiences or in observing the *how to* and the *what if* of my teachings?"

This time, I used my mind and overrode my growling stomach.

"I see a rotten log," I said. "I smell something that means food. I hear and feel some vibrations of creatures that are probably at work on that log. That puts an image of lunch in my mind. I shall go to that log, turn it over, and see if my image is right, and I shall find lunch, if I am right. If not, I shall try other ways of foraging for food." (You see, I had really learned from the morning's experiences.)

"Now," added my mother, "you are dealing in Ideas—the great *what ifs*. You are on the way to solving a problem or challenge.

"You will be no ordinary bear; you shall be a *thinking bear*. You probably will meet very few other creatures who really think, or use imagination, or deal in Ideas; but if you do, you will fulfill your destiny as a Special Bear, whatever destiny that is to be."

So, one colossal swat by a very wise mother changed my life. When we returned from lunching and munching, my mother reported to my father that I was ready. And so I was, for whatever was my next step in growing up.

CHAPTER 3

SON OF ALTHAR

My next step, almost literally, was to be invited to walk with my father. My father chose to share his time and his counsel with me, sharing his vision and wisdom, his hopes and dreams as well as all his skills and strengths. He was strong, yet kind and gentle, as only the truly strong can be.

At this time, my father was so old and respected that he was no longer required to be competitive. He was acknowledged as the unchallenged power-force in the kingdom, choosing his own counsel and company and use of time. That he would choose me, as well as my mother, to share ideas was not typical of our species, but we were, admittedly, *different.* I was to be educated in a special and different way.

My father was known as Althar the Wise, and I loved listening and learning in his presence. I was taught about heavenly as well as earthly legends and myths, about the powers of the earth and sky under the dominion of the One and Only Great Spirit—the Divine Source that made and activated the universe! (Pretty heavy stuff for a young bear just out of rotten logs, grubs, and a mind-set of never-ending *lunch*!)

Time, my father explained to me on one of our Sharing Walks, was very long; life was very short. Sometimes one particular life, one special individual would be singled out to step away from the usual path of the species or tribe. My father called that usual path the "*ordinary life cycle of feed and breed.*"

This special individual would be given the chance to carry a different message, to fulfill a different destiny. This messenger would carry a 'Light', so to speak, he or she would pursue an idea, and perhaps you could call it a Great Truth. My father called it 'The Great What If?' He believed that all other thoughts, truths, ideas (what ifs?) would flow into the ultimate Big Idea, the Divine Idea from which all Truths originated and to which all Truths returned.

Now, if that boggles your mind, think what it did to a youngster bear just growing up into life, doing fun and playful things, and just beginning to entertain heavy thoughts and ideas, and whose greatest idea a few days ago concerned lunch. (Who, thereafter, called all food occasions: Lunch.)

I had not the slightest clue as to what much of my father's lessons were trying to tell me, but I respected and treasured his wisdom. I tucked away all his instructions in a special corner of my mind to be considered later—and, hopefully, understood in context of other experience and wisdom. I did follow a 'Light', as you will see!

My father and I shared our walks in late afternoons and evenings. I slept later (or didn't sleep) on a head rattling around with wisdom and ideas.

I spent mornings, usually with my mother asking questions and getting ideas sorted out. We shared lunch. She was amazingly skillful at 'lunch'—and her talents in food-foraging were the equal of my father's idea-foraging.

I, obviously, was being brought up in a different way from any others of my family. I was never a typical Great Brown Bear—nor were my parents. I did not find my differentness (nor theirs) at all troubling. I rather enjoyed it, and all their attentions. I certainly relished my special life as it unfolded every day, and I took very little thought of the future.

However, one very still, clear night in early autumn, that easy, beautiful, and protected life changed forever. That night, I grew up. Fast!

I was left alone. My father and mother had turned me out of their lives and into my own.

The lovely night, the radiant stars, the familiar embracing forests were all there, as they had always been, yet everything had changed for me. My home was no longer home and probably never would be again.

My future, my destiny, was in the power of my commitment—and the power of the Star.

Book II

The Journey of the Star—South

Chapter 1

Outbound to Exotic Lands and Creatures

I stood unmoving in that starlit meadow for what felt like forever. I simply could not take in all that had happened to me in the course of one night. My brain was numb but my heart felt like it had broken in irreparable pieces.

In most animal societies, young males leave their home community to form their own. But I was so sure of my special status as not-an-ordinary bear that I had never given any thought about leaving home, or about where I was really going—and why.

How long I stood there in shock, frozen in thought and movement, I don't know. Gradually I became aware of a warm, comforting glow in my paw. It was the Star-Stone bringing me back into life.

Overhead, my Star of Mystery bathed me in its radiance. I moved slowly at first, but then, with growing confidence to the south. Across the meadow, into the dark heart of the forest, I followed the white threads of light that moved with me through the trees.

With that confidence, came the gradual recall of my father's last instructions; warmth and resolution flowed through me in the strength and grandeur of those words.

I realized that my calling—my purpose—in the Light of the Star (if for no other reason or result) was to live out those words in every day and every step of my Journey.

A bear, a supposedly ferocious, powerful beast, was sent out to be a 'Bearer of Peace'? What an incredible dream! What an impossible commission! No. I believed in myself; I believed in my Star!

For many days I walked south, following the Star at night, the Star-Stone during daylight. Food and water were plentiful, and as I was so young and strong, I found little need for sleep or rest. My self-confidence increased day by day.

I gradually recovered from the sorrow and shock of being on my own, and I found that I had all the survival skills I needed to make it. In fact, I became a little incautious with my new self-confidence.

The area through which I walked seemed wild and empty of other creatures. I supposed that if any other animals noted my presence, I was being given a wide berth. I was, after all, very large and strong-looking, and bears were considered the top of the power structure.

Suddenly, one day, I realized I was not alone. I sensed a shadowy presence, or presences, unseen, but felt, on either side and in back of me.

I felt a chill of apprehension and called out for recognition, to no avail. The shadowing persisted for days, despite my challenges for identification. No one came near me, and there was no threat from the shadows. But I knew I was not traveling alone anymore. Finally in the advancing twilight of one day, I halted in a small clearing and slowly turned in a circle, trying to face down and challenge my shadows.

"Whoever you are, please reply to my request for recognition. I am Althazar, son of King Althar of the Northern Forests. I am only passing through this territory, and if I have left my own kingdom and am now in yours, I ask your leave to pass through harmlessly.

"I am on a special Journey south, and request safe passage to only feed on berries and nuts and drink on my way. I seek no land, nor power, nor any conflict. You have been my companions for days. Please meet me face-to-face that we may share this Journey more amicably."

It seemed a civil, if not rather formal request for diplomatic relations to be opened. My father had always taught me that civility and courtesy in all relations were paramount in kingship, as was respect for others. But I felt a bit stuffy in my first effort to open dialogue—especially with shadows.

Suddenly, the shadows materialized! I was surrounded by a pack of wild wolves! I sat down as a gesture of peace, and they too, sat in a circle around me.

What happened next, I soon learned, was in no way typical of a pack of wolves encountering a lone stranger in their territory.

The largest wolf addressed me: "I am Lanthar, king of this land through which you journey. This is my family. We mean you no harm, but as you must recognize, we are wary of strangers. Welcome, Prince Althazar. Pass in peace."

With the formalities over, Lanthar proceeded to introduce his family to me—a family that continued to increase, as more and more wolves came out of the shadows to encircle me.

By the time I had acknowledged each wolf around the circle once, the formality of the scene had changed to easy hilarity, as I mangled name after name. I discovered that wolves had a keen sense of humor and sense of fun, as well as easy camaraderie.

Our visiting went on late into the night, as I was plied with question after question, especially after I told them about the Star and the Star-Stone, and my Journey into the Great Unknown. I learned that wolves generally range across wide areas and are great hunters because of their need for pack coordination. But they seldom fully leave home, so to speak.

So my Journey of the Star awed them, especially because it was a lone journey. The idea of life as 'a lone wolf' did not appeal to them—well, there was an exception.

One very large and handsome young wolf named Lothar (one name I could not only remember, but pronounce) questioned me at great length. He seemed fascinated by the Star and the prospect of a Journey into the Great Unknown.

"Althazar," he asked, "would you consider a traveling companion, a partner in your adventure? I am large and strong and very skilled in trail-knowledge—and the absence of one wolf from this large pack would not impose any hardship."

He looked seriously and earnestly at his father who, after a long thoughtful silence, gave his blessing to his son—if it was a plan that I agreed to.

I thought it was a splendid idea. I was getting a bit tired of only a star and a rock for companionship, even if both were mystical and magical.

What remained of the night was spent in leave-taking, an emotional frenzy of a large and very close family—something that was completely alien to me, raised as an only child. I marveled at such exuberant and unrestrained behavior, and did wonder why, if Lothar was so deep in ties to a close family, he chose to leave and become a loner like me?

CHAPTER 2

LOTHAR

That question was pretty well answered by the time Lothar and I made our exit late the next day. The wolves were exceedingly emotional, and the energy and vocalization expended in their brother's departure wore me out. Too much of a good thing was exhausting! We took off in an easy lope, followed for a while by part of the family. Apparently, Lothar's father and mother had made their farewells sometime during the night, because they did not follow us.

I wondered if Lothar had received as serious a send-off as I had. I asked him as we proceeded out of his kingdom. He said the expectations and behavior instructions were, indeed, serious and thought-provoking. I repeated my father's exhortations to me. Lothar nodded seriously and said, "It is a heavy responsibility that we carry, you and I." Then a sparkle of humor returned to his eyes. "I think the challenge of a Journey into the Great Unknown is marvelous. It is certainly more exciting a prospect than puppy-training (the job of number two wolf) or waiting to possibly inherit from my father. I think both he and I knew that I was a bit different from the rest of the clan and would never really fit into its society."

So, both Lothar and I were different and, seemingly, were destined to follow our own Star of Destiny—a very exciting prospect to both of us.

We loped along steadily, ever southward, guided by the Star low in the south at night, and the Star-Stone by day. Being young and strong, we slept little. We paused only for short naps and food.

Because of our autumn departure and our southward movement, the abundance of a rich harvest was still around us. While winter might be close on our heels, we had ample berries, nuts and other vegetation in our countryside. That is, I did. Lothar was a meat-eater and had to forage for his own sustenance.

Early in our relationship, he had surmised that I was not so much a predator as a forager, and he, in reluctance to give me any discomfort, did his food-getting out of my sight or sound. But, thoughtfully, he was quick to put me on to any nuts or berries he spotted.

This was a gentle side to a wolf that I didn't expect. Lothar seemed to be always surprising me by his sensitivity and courtesy, his ready impishness, sense of humor, and loyalty—to an extreme.

The grin that Lothar was ready to share would have frozen any other creature by its show of teeth, but I quickly caught on to his good nature—and that wolf's grin.

He was full of high spirits, optimism, and curiosity. Our adventure into the Great Unknown was the answer to his dream as well as mine. I had never had so sure an understanding of life as the unsurety of this adventure. Lothar and I were made for each other as Companions of the Star.

In growing ease and enjoyment, we two friends gradually made our way south. The star rose ever so imperceptibly in the south as we progressed. Every clear night it was always on the same bearing, and so were we. It led; we followed.

Time, to an animal, is measured in light and dark, but mostly in seasons. As we moved southward, seasons and climates changed. Landforms and vegetation changed, and although we were always conscious that we were passing through the lands and territories of many different creatures, we seldom crossed paths with any that disputed our passage.

I never met another bear, and Lothar never met another wolf. Although, on many a chill night we heard them at a distance. Wolves, it seems, have a vast vocal repertoire and communicate across great distances. Whatever Lothar said as we traveled, it was sufficient to let us pass in peace. That, in itself, was just one more miracle of our Journey.

We were fortunate to always find nourishment of some kind, enough to grow to our prime and full size, trail-hardy and resourceful. I was a very large bear and Lothar was a very large wolf. Together, we probably looked truly awesome, although we always meant to move nonaggressively, in peace. Seasons came and went, and our route flattened out away from mountains and forests. We tried to follow south-flowing river systems that supported water and vegetation. Rivers, however, often seemed to wander, and so did we.

One early evening the scent of smoke put us in a sense of alarm! Smoke, fire—to a wild animal, they meant danger. We were downwind of whatever was burning, but as we saw no glow or flames, we hoped it was safe to investigate. We went quite a distance before coming to the edge of a high bluff. We looked down at a broad valley that had strange little humps evenly spaced around small fires. Even stranger were the sights, sounds and smells coming from that area. There were many small herds of stocky beasts with horns, as well as other smaller woolly ones, and many noisy wolf-like creatures that barked and yipped around in confusion.

The strangest looking of all were hind-leg walking creatures in loose, flapping course hides. These animals seemed to make endlessly curious sounds of communication within their packs.

Lothar and I looked at one another in amazement and awe.

"Who, and what, are these creatures?" I whispered. Although none could have possibly heard me above the chaos.

"I can't even guess," Lothar replied, "but I have a feeling that they are harmful. Let's get out of here before the wind changes and they get our scent."

We ran off in a downwind direction, putting distance and woods between us. We didn't stop until deep darkness slowed us and all trace of smoke disappeared.

We decided to rest a while and talk about what we had encountered. Lothar had dined on some unfortunate rodent, and I found a cache of very spicy insects—all of which would hold us until later.

I mused, "Father told me that I would encounter many strange and exotic lands and creatures—and I have a notion that we have just scratched the surface of *strange*!"

"Strange, I accept," said my companion, "but do you think that these two-legged creatures are called *exotics*?"

"For lack of a better name, let's say that we have encountered our first tribe of exotics," I replied. "Not to offer offense, old friend," I continued, "exotics are even more noisy and vocal than wolves."

Lothar laughed and agreed heartily. "They don't smell as pretty, though."

I left it at that. It was too dark to see, at that moment, but I felt Lothar's wonderfully wicked wolf's grin!

CHAPTER 3

GREYL

As we wandered our way south, we encountered more rivers that bent to the west. We swam quite a few that were not going our way. As we were both strong swimmers, this was not a major inconvenience but, then, none of the rivers was a major crossing.

"If," said Lothar, "most of the waterways are turning west, it would be reasonable to assume they are draining into a major body of water, don't you think?"

"I think you're right," I replied, having come to the same conclusion. "I wonder if it will be a big barrier at sometime?"

It would be a short time until our questions would be answered—and then, in rather strange, almost miraculous ways (and means).

We were traveling in lush, marshy lands, with a hill or two from which to survey the territory. We saw or smelled more of those tribes (or clusters, to be more precise) of exotics. We gave them wide berth, and, as their scent was so recognizable, we were given a long warning of their territory.

We went from hill to hill, or if a high enough hill was not available, I climbed any available tall tree to set a safe course. Tree-climbing was easy and fun for me, but as the trees were not very big, I often had a fast ride down, as the supple trunks could not handle my weight and bent in a rapid arc to the ground.

Lothar found that sight hilarious and wished he could have a ride too. At the sight of me, he would laugh so hard that he would roll around on his back with his feet pedaling in the air. Now, I thought that was hilarious!

One day, when we were indulging in some playful and noisy antics, we heard, over our laughter, another series of even stranger noises. The sound seemed to come from a nearby thicket.

We searched for the source of the sound, poking around through the brush and foliage in vain.

"Onk, onk," came the sound again. "Up here, you useless, silly groundlings." At that, we looked up and saw a strange sight—a large, very large bird caught upside down at the top of a slender, tall tree.

The bird was thrashing around wildly, hanging by one leg, wings and feathers flaying around futilely.

"Aah," Lothar drooled, "dinner!" His amber eyes glowed like coals.

"Oh, for goodness sake, Lothar, don't even think that. Any one in danger or trouble demands help and courtesy, not devouring!" I countered. I immediately caught the wink in Lothar's amber eye. He knew how I felt about killing—at least in my sight. But Lothar was a frightful tease!

"Mr. Bird," I shouted above the confusion, "Stop thrashing around and maybe we can find a way to get you down—and release you!"

"I am a Mrs.—and I am a Goose—and even being quickly eaten might be better than slowly starving to death up here!"

Lothar mumbled something like: "My thoughts exactly," but I gave him a quick swat on his head, and he gave me another wink.

We sat down to better consider the situation and also to better see the goose. I felt introductions were in order, now that the goose and we had settled down.

"I am Prince Althazar of the Northern Forests…and this is Prince Lothar of the Middle Forests—and we are on a special Journey of the Star into the Great Unknown."

The goose, although still at the disadvantage of being upside down, very thin, very rumpled and shucking off feathers, still had her own presence of dignity in the fire of coal black eyes that seemed to bore right through us.

"I am Greyl," she replied with a certain haughtiness, (which I had noticed of all winged creatures) "and I am of the lowlands of the salt marshes who has lost her mate—and seeks him everywhere. A sudden windstorm grounded me days ago, and I blundered into this animal snare, set by those ghastly two-legged, wingless hunters called Humans!"

Neither Lothar nor I quite understood her references to any of this, but we were to find out quite soon.

"Perhaps," continued Greyl, still infinitely polite but cool, "we could get on with some actions more than courteous words?"

Lothar replied, "Zar, if you would lean on that tree, it would bend over, and then I could bite through that tether and free the goose. What do you think?"

"Of course," I concurred, "my weight should ease it over and bring Greyl to the ground." Then I added softly, so that only Lothar could hear, "You won't harm her, will you, old friend?"

"No, no, no," Lothar said, "I wouldn't think of it. Besides why would such a noble beast as myself think of consuming a thin, old, stringy bird like her?" Again those amber eyes of Lothar glowed, this time, I hoped, in good humor and honest, good intentions!

Lothar got up and positioned himself where he hoped Greyl would come down, (keenly aware of those piercing black eyes, no doubt). I went over and backed into the tall sapling that tethered Greyl.

I was in very fit shape, heavily in my prime, and that sapling was no match for my weight slowly pinning it to the ground.

"Hold it there Zar…she's down. Now to bite through the tether." It seemed like ages, but finally, Lothar said, "I've done it—now wait until we've both gotten clear—and remember to step aside fast. That tree may whip back up and spank you!" Spank was hardly the action word for what happened next, when Lothar yelled "Clear!"

I jumped fast, but the tree was faster—and whip was an understatement. That thing hit me on the rump so fast and with such a vengeance that I was tumbled feet-over-ears through the thickets and brush, plowing a path down the hill like a boulder in an avalanche.

I came to rest flat on my back, but hardly knew it because my world was still spinning around and around, sun and stars orbiting inside my aching head. I was vaguely aware of Lothar crashing and yelping after me. Whether in laughter or alarm, I only realized when he landed on my stomach and started to lick my face, whines and cries included. It was the first time I had ever seen Lothar afraid, and realized how much we apparently meant to one another. But his concerns and affection were noisy and wet, and I tried to gently push him off my stomach so I could catch my breath and senses.

At that moment, there were at least half a dozen of Lothar whirling around in my vision, as well as spinning explosions of stars.

Lothar slid off me only to be replaced by a very distraught Greyl, who, shedding feathers—and cries of her own—landed on me to express *her* concern.

"It's all my fault—my fault," she squawked. "I've killed you—and you're just trying to save me! I'm so sorry, so sorry…oh, oh, oh…!"

I limply raised a shaky paw to brush Greyl off my stomach, "Enough, enough…I certainly appreciate your concern, but just let me lie here quietly and regain my senses."

I realized that Lothar and Greyl were now sitting side-by-side in rapt attention to my every movement—some kind of miraculous truce had been struck between them. It was a moment to treasure, and probably a first! (Actually, for the rest of Lothar's and Greyl's relationship, they really enjoyed an adversarial posture of threats and insults, but it took me a long while to realize that!)

Animals in the wild are seldom given any time to recover from injury, and I was up and about very soon. Although, at the time, it seemed like ages passed while my senses restored. I was overjoyed to find, upon arising that all moving parts got up with me. Although I was thoroughly rattled and bruised, I wasn't broken. My joy in functioning again was matched by Lothar's and Greyl's.

Lothar smiled that wicked wolf grin and said, "Had a nice trip, did we?"

I aimed a swat at his ears, but missed, due to a certain continuing lack of coordination. We slowly toiled up the hill to sit and survey the area for a brief rest. (The goose of course, flew up, but she was about as uncoordinated as was I, right then.)

I leaned against a soft hummock of grass, Lothar stretched out beside me, his head on his front paws. The goose stood warily on a small mound of dirt, which she probably hoped was over a wolf-pounce away. She was anything but in a resting mode, even after her long ordeal. She said, abruptly, "How can two natural enemies be friends?"

Lothar rose up and met my glance, "How can two natural friends be enemies?" he countered, in his sometimes too-direct way. "This lumbering, *fur* mountain came into our kingdom one day—seasons ago—bearing dignity, friendliness, and peace. Now, any sizable pack of wolves can tear apart any one animal, regardless of size. But this animal, this bear, had something about him so different; it was intriguing, compelling, and curious—even to a cut-throat pack as we were. My father welcomed him and we all exchanged introductions.

"Then we heard his story, of his miraculous Star, and his Journey into a complete Great Unknown!

"Such a wild idea, such an unrealistic dream caught my fancy—and I joined up with what you call my natural enemy to become Brothers in the Journey of the Star.

"Now, can you, Mrs. Goose, understand any of this?"

Greyl looked intently at Lothar and me, those black beady eyes skewering us both in turn. After a long silence, she said, "Tell me more: especially about the

Star and the Journey. We geese have rather special connections with both. And, Mr. Dog Breath, don't be sarcastic or patronizing of me, I've seen more of this world by wing than you'll ever see trotting over it on your four, splayed paws!"

Lothar rolled over on his back, laughed, and howled at this exchange. "Truce, truce," he called between his bouts of laughter. "Dog Breath to Bird Brain: I've met my match. I give up! We three natural enemies can be mutual friends.

"I shall tease you, I'll probably trade insults with you, but I shall listen to you and I shall never eat you! I never eat anyone who can trade intelligent and humorous conversation with me! And, Althazar, tell our new partner all about your Star and our mysterious Journey into, over, and through heavens-knows-what!"

So I did, recounting everything from the start to present. Greyl was very attentive and asked many questions, all of which indicated a quick and intelligent mind and curiosity. I never gave much thought to bird wisdom, but I found that goose wisdom was truly awesome. Geese, indeed, traveled great distances and adapted to many different challenges. Unlike many lesser animals that only lived by instinct, apparently, geese could learn and modify behavior by experience, and they had unusual memories and forms of communication, as well.

I believe Greyl's wisdom, reasoning ability, and skills in observation even impressed Lothar deeply, because it was he who realized how valuable she could be in mapping out our movement south and in warning us of danger. Our keen sense of smell and hearing, coupled with Greyl's keen eyesight and aerial reports could really insure a safer and more efficient journey.

We all agreed it was, indeed, a lucky day when we met and formed our new partnership.

"Oh," added Lothar, "by the way, what is a dog?"

CHAPTER 4

SOUTH BY THE GREAT INLAND SEA

It did not take Lothar and me many days to wonder how we had made it this far without Greyl's help. Her overhead view, spotting the best routes and even looking for forage for me, made her partnership invaluable. Some of our Journey had indeed proved a little lean for me, and my fur suit was a little loose after we left forested land for the steppes.

Greyl's wisdom and knowledge of the area made even Lothar sorry he had labeled her Bird Brain, but she seemed to enjoy insulting banter, so he kept it up. When she explained Dogs to us, he thought he had gotten the worst of the exchange. (Not that he didn't deserve it!)

"Dogs," explained Greyl, "are wolves that have adopted humans, or what you call exotics. A long time ago, dogs, apparently, had decided to come in from the wild and hunt with humans, or for them."

Lothar gave a snort of derision. "Why?"

Greyl continued, ignoring Lothar's stiff-legged pacing back and forth and his huffing and snorting. "Maybe for food, warmth, companionship. After all, both wolves and humans are pack animals and have a strong social structure. Maybe a lost puppy was taken in and tamed…who knows? It was a long time ago. Maybe you will have a chance to ask one of them. And don't snarl at me…I'm only the messenger! And also, I have no great love for dogs. They and humans hunt and kill waterfowl."

Hoping to divert further dissent or ire, I said, "Well, now we've disposed of dogs, by agreeing that they are wayward wolves. What about humans, those exotics?"

Greyl continued, though keeping one eye on our wolf while addressing me. "Now that is a complicated subject—humans. I know they come in many sizes, appearances, and live in communities. As they are a predatory animal, I am leery of them. They are clever and ruthless killers, but I have flown over vast communities of them, living in complicated and permanent structures. About the only thing I see in common is that they walk upright on two legs, and their front legs have very dexterous paws with fingers that they use to make tools and structures and anything they need.

"Oh yes, humans are very social, communicating in complex language and expressions with both their hands and voices. They talk a lot—they sing, they dance, they even laugh.

"They appear weak and puny compared to other predators, but they seem to be very intelligent to make up for being physically weak. And they think and reason. I know because that snare I was caught in was cleverly crafted, you might say. And I have seen my kinfolk caught in very big and complicated traps, like webs.

"Humans are powerful, in ways we animals cannot fully understand. So, be wary. There may be much to fear, but also, there may be much to learn from them. They are, I believe, very wise.

"They may look and smell strange to us, but maybe they think we do too!" (She cocked her head at Lothar.)

Greyl was making a real effort of being fair to both dogs and humans. As I found all through my Journey, the most wise of creatures among us were those who tried to inform and comment from various perspectives and viewpoints in the fairest way they knew.

Greyl might qualify as a Bird Brain, but that little head was packed with wisdom, perspective, and information. Lothar agreed with my estimation after he got over his huffing and snorting act.

We quickly fell into an easy routine: Lothar and I fed and napped in a well-hidden covert during the daylight, Greyl fed and scouted at the same time. We met at dusk to plan our Journey during the darkness. Greyl would sleep during the night and after our meeting. Apparently, she had no trouble spotting us after we finished our night's trek.

During our evening social hour, we learned many facts and observations from our well-traveled scout. We learned that the vast stretch of water on our west (which we were paralleling to the south) was a great salt sea. From Greyl's point of view, the flight was many days long, but only a day's flight wide. The sea was shallow and marshy to the north, deep and bordered by a great mountain range to the south. Big rivers drained into it from the north and only some drained from the mountains.

The sea was rich with fish and waterfowl, which drew humans to its resources. Greyl had flown over all the migration area sites that she described—and many others to the north. She had abandoned them when she lost her mate, choosing instead to stay in the Great Inland Sea year-round.

It was quite humbling to Lothar and to me to realize that there was a great deal more land in our world than any earthbound animal could ever see. If we had wings—oh, what we could see…where we could go!

Perhaps this great range of life that a creature like Greyl could traverse deserved the haughtiness and farsighted look that birds seemed to project. I had judged birds to affect an annoying superiority—now I knew why, and I began to understand and certainly envy them!

Our Journey, though probably long at this time, was very easy and enjoyable, although we encountered many detours around inlets and marshes and other obstacles. With our amicable spotter, we progressed successfully.

I suggested that Greyl ride on my back at night instead of flying to water-areas for her naps. She flew up on my shoulders to give the idea a try; but my lumbering gait—bears walk with both legs moving together on their respective sides—made her slide off (and seasick!).

Lothar was so amused by our antics that he lay on his back and pedaled his legs in the air—a sight that always gave both Greyl and me great amusement. A seasick goose? laughed Lothar.

Greyl and I agreed that this was an idea whose time had not come, and she and we went back to our original routine.

One time I asked Greyl if she could take us to an area to see if I could catch some of the fish that she said swarmed in this sea. Bears are very good fishers—at least some are. I was quite expert, although I was averse to killing other animals. I made an exception to fish (bears can and do eat practically anything—I was just a bit choosy.)

I knew I had to fatten up with good staying-power food if we were to undertake a great mountain range in the future. Lothar was very good at supplying his own food, and had been, all during our many seasons together. I, however, had to munch many more nuts and green stuff to get the same energy as a meat-eater. Fish would certainly be packed with power for me!

The stream mouth that Greyl led us to was, indeed, swarming with fish. I could not believe my eyes, and just stood back and marveled for a moment.

Not so Lothar! Upon seeing an unbelievable food resource in front of him, he gave a yelp of ecstasy and leaped stiff-legged into the pool in front of him. (This pouncing technique was very effective in hunting—pinning down a small rodent on land. It did not work under water, especially if one was unsure of the water's depth!)

Both the fish and Lothar disappeared at the splash. The fish were not pinned down, and the water was far deeper than Lothar expected.

Greyl gave a honk of surprise, and I just sat down and began to rock with laughter. Lothar could amuse me with his wolf antics as much as I amused him with mine. Luckily, we both had a quick and ripe sense of humor.

Lothar surfaced, spluttering—obviously without a fish or his dignity. He hauled out, not too near to us, shook vigorously all the while avoiding our eyes, but with a meaningful curl of his lip.

I couldn't resist it. I said, sarcastically: "Had a nice trip, did we?"

Lothar didn't answer but ran off to a grassy area to roll himself dry and fluff up his fur suit (as well as his dignity).

Greyl and I were still laughing when she suggested an aerial view might relocate the fish. I concurred: "Just watch your shadow—fish are easily spooked by sudden shadows."

Greyl was soon back. "The fish have swarmed downstream—obviously away from this spot. It just depends on how deep you fish. Is your style above, or under the water?"

We moved our position downstream to shallower water.

My style was slow and patient, standing very quietly in the stream until the fish got used to me and even got intrigued by the movement of my fur in the water. Then…wop! I would scoop one out of the water onto the bank before the rest even knew what happened.

"Onk!" exclaimed Greyl as the first fish whizzed by her head and, still flopping, hit the bank. Then two, three, four more, faster than one can grasp!

"Lothar," I called, "quit skulking and sulking. We have more fish than we can handle. Come back and share this feast!"

Greyl, of course, could not participate but could only dodge and get out of range of flying *fish*! I have to admit the success of my style wasn't always this dramatic, and naturally, I was enjoying my moment of showing off!

Lothar joined the show, still avoiding my eyes, but I hardly noticed because my attention was on other things.

Lothar and I ate fish until we could gorge no more. (Animals in the wild have to eat as much as they can hold whenever they have the chance, because chances may be far apart.)

When we finished for the day, I swept the remaining fish back into the water where they seemed to recover, no worse for their *outing*. I can't recall any other time when I had to give back fish because I caught so many.

Needless to say, Lothar and I slept for a few days in a nearby covert. Greyl, shaking her head, impressed and amazed, flew off hoping to be as fortunate in abundant food. We did not move on for days, returning as often as possible to put away as much energy as we could store. I was better off than Lothar, as bears can store a lot more bulk than wolves and, when food is scarce, can live off their reserves for long periods of time.

Wolves burn energy constantly, being very wary and active at all times and have to eat more frequently, but no one has ever heard of a fat wolf, but a fat *bear*? Ah, well—you know!

I continued to catch many fish as we finally started again moving south, parallel to the Great Inland Sea. The fish there were unused to bears, I guess, or else there were just too many of them. Greyl seemed to know all the best of the fishing holes, and we ate our way south until we could see the great mountain range, that she had spoken of, rising ominously ahead.

Lothar returned to his dignity and good humor, even as he thanked me for feast after feast. I told him we should never know when he might have to return the favor—that the joy of partnership was in caring for one another, for the good of each. The success of any communal venture depended on teamwork, a tactic all too natural to a wolf, of course. The two of us—and now three—were a team.

With Greyl spotting our Journey from the air, we avoided any contact with humans, and arrived at the narrow plain that footed the southern end of the Great Inland Sea and the high mountains rising above it.

I knew that our delightfully easy trip was about to end, and challenges of another kind were right in our face. The Star still pointed us to the south, and it was up to us to find a route that honored that commitment, high mountains not withstanding.

CHAPTER 5

THE GREAT BARRIER MOUNTAINS

We stayed in the shadow of those awesome barriers for quite a while, during which time Greyl did an aerial search for ways through and over. She said she had never flown over the mountains, not that she could not, but that her natural habitat was on the shores of her sea. Now, she was as curious as were we about possible routes and about what lay beyond.

Lothar and I could not even imagine how we would possibly continue on our Journey south without a bird's eye view of our route, a view that Greyl had taken on as her *mission*!

She had returned to sleekness and vigor and renewed purpose for her life. Her period of mourning and depression had been replaced by a new sense of belonging.

Her words of long-past were recalled often by Lothar and me: "How can natural enemies be mutual friends?" The answers lay in my father's words of even longer ago—Respect, Understanding, and Peaceful Intent. So far, we had never met any creatures that meant us ill, and we went at our lives each day with an attitude of wonder and joy, in the sure expectation of finding such, as well as the openness that recognized miracles all along our way.

We fattened up on great quantities of fish, which, commented Lothar..."threatened to overcome our natural wolf and bear aroma."

Greyl disagreed, "Wolf by any other diet is still 'dog breath' to me."

Lothar replied, "I have run out of insults, but I am working on growing wings and gills, and that should knock her feathers off!"

While the feasting and the route-searching went on, we had leisurely time to visit and exchange ideas—those great thoughts that asked "*what if*"?

Greyl was the one with the most questions. Lothar and I had already explored many of our own questions along our Journey, but questions and answers never truly stop.

"What if," asked Greyl, "you come to the end of your Journey and there is no there, there?"

"Well," I drawled, trying to frame an answer that didn't have too many theres, there. "When you, Greyl, find a very succulent head of grain and you eat it and everything is over and you have nothing left except a bare stalk, do you feel you have not reached your goal? Or, that you have been cheated?"

Lothar cut in while Greyl was digesting my reply. "Oh, I like that, After a very satisfying meal, when there is nothing left but the memory, one still has a glorious taste in the mouth and a feeling of having fed well—both body and spirit. Yes, yes…I like that!"

I nodded. "There are different kinds of goals to reach for. But in our Journey, no ends, goals, or achievements were ever promised—just the Journey itself and all the Unknowns to meet along the way. '*What ifs*' deal with the Idea of the next event to come, or that which could come. It is almost impossible for most animals to understand the Idea of the future, living, as it were, almost exclusively on instinct, in the present.

"The fact that the three of us can even explore or understand something that hasn't happened yet is truly remarkable. The world of Ideas is limited to few of our species; but perhaps there are other creatures in the world who deal easily and naturally with Ideas. Greyl, you said exotics, err, humans seemed to be ever in communication with their fellows. Do you believe that their species might be able to work with the world of Ideas?"

She replied, "Yes, perhaps that is their great strength and their means of survival. Maybe they are a true *thinking* species."

I mused on. "I wonder if we few animals who think and can deal with ideas can ever communicate with humans. Do you believe there is a bridge we might find or build between us? I wonder if their species is ready to seek Peace, to seek communication among all creatures. Or, is this little dream of us few, only a dream of a few and, maybe, too far ahead of our time? What if humans can't even build Peace among humans?"

Lothar added, "Personally, I'm wary of them from what I've seen and from what Greyl reports. We can barely handle our Ideas; maybe humans have the same trouble. Maybe humans wouldn't truly want to *listen* to animals!"

Greyl added a final comment, "Only if you listen can you begin to understand, and only in understanding can you begin to respect others, but it all seems to start with Peace. Maybe our Journey really is living out Peace and in that climate all other '*what ifs*' are possible."

That seems to be our Journey, I thought to myself—full of miracles and exchanges of wonder, but both a means and an end in itself: just like Peace, a climate in which all Ideas and creatures may grow and prosper, as Greyl so wisely noted.

* * * *

So, on to the mountains—and the reality of our Journey at hand. Now it was more a question of "*how to*," not "*what if*"!

Greyl, now, was constantly on the wing, enjoying her new sense of importance and connection to a new family. Lothar and I moved slowly along the coastal plain, heading west to where Greyl said the mountains were less awesome. We all hoped she would find a way over them that we could attempt…and survive.

We had begun to spend as much time as possible in cool areas so that we would not lose our winter coats, which, we knew, we would definitely need for our mountain crossing. It was currently late spring and we hoped the coming of regional summer would keep the passes open, assuming that Greyl could find one.

Greyl plopped into our thicket one evening, so full of excitement that we knew she had found something significant.

"I believe I've found a way for you—I've talked to a couple of very canny mountain goats who have shown me a passage, known but to them!"

Lothar and I said, in unison, "What are canny mountain goats?" We were wondering if these animals were more of the strange or *exotics.*

"Oh," replied Greyl, "You've probably not seen their kind before. They are white, shaggy, four-legged animals about the size of a deer, with split hooves for mountain climbing. They live above the timberline on rocks and crags, eating whatever vegetation grows at such heights. Very shy and wary creatures, but curious. I made contact with them because of their curiosity of a large, winged non-predator (like me) who flew down from the clouds onto their home grounds.

"Oh, yes, they have small, spiky horns and shaggy beards and very quizzical, curious eyes. And I do believe that their legs on one side must be shorter than on the other side to adjust for always being on mountain slopes!"

I poked Lothar who seemed about to make some smart remark on that last statement of Greyl's, keeping my own "Oh?" to myself. Greyl was so happy about her success, it would be unmannerly to be anything but equally enthusiastic. We were, and said so.

"Will these, err, uh, canny-mountain 'ghosts' guide us over the mountains or point us to trails or what?" I asked. (Greyl smiled at the mispronunciation.)

"I'm going back to ask them," replied Greyl. "They are such wary, shy creatures, I don't know what they will do, especially as they look on a bear and a wolf as predators. I told them of my initial feelings and concerns, and I said if you two wouldn't eat a choice, succulent bird as me, why would you go after stringy old goats like them?

"Of course, I didn't say it quite as insulting as that. Anyway, they politely said that they would think about all this. They really were very nice. Maybe there is something to this business of Peaceful Intent. It all seems amazing, if not miraculous to me."

Lothar and I nodded in agreement.

"Do these mountain 'ghosts' have names?" I asked.

She nodded: "The closest I could come to pronouncing their names is Caprior and Caprious. Which is which, I can't tell. They seem to be twins and talk in a sort of sequence, as if the one knows exactly what the other is to say next. It is like seeing double and hearing double all in one. Does any of this make sense?"

I nodded.

Lothar shook his head.

Greyl just laughed: "Ghosts indeed!" she exclaimed.

CHAPTER 6

MOUNTAIN GHOSTS

While Greyl was completing the details of our Journey at higher altitudes, Lothar and I were beginning our Journey at lower altitudes. Greyl had sent us to a river valley that led upwards into the mountains, along a route that promised water and forage until timberline, at least. After that, the promise of a trail over and through was to depend on our allies-to-be: the mountain 'ghosts'. Our trust, as well as our lives, rested in their skills and commitment...and we had yet to meet them!

Actually, we never did meet them eye-to-eye, although we were to hear them—and sense their presence—and follow their trails. It was almost like following the Star, except we did see hoof prints and scuff marks pointing the directions. We did feel the presence of shadowy 'ghosts' and we did smell them! There was never any real doubt where their trails were!

It was summer and the river was full of winter-melt water. Forage was available. The climb became steeper every day as we gained altitude. We moved by day for safety—there certainly were no harmful creatures to threaten us—and we did need to see where we were going. The air grew colder, and the view grew more spectacular with every step. We used every clearing to pause and rest and to admire the spread of the countryside below us.

"Just think," I commented between huffs and puffs, "this is the way Greyl sees the world all the time! No wonder winged creatures are so special. The land is so very interesting and beautiful looking down at it."

Lothar replied, when he caught his breath, "We can now see the coastal plain around this end of the Great Inland Sea—and look, we can really see both shores. There *is* a far shore. What a sight!"

Lothar was still gasping for breath, and I said: "Well, good buddy, we are really out of shape, aren't we? Too long in the lowlands."

"Lowlands, nothing," snorted my companion. "Short of breath from long of FISH! You said no one had ever seen a fat wolf. Well, look at one! I've bulked up so mightily on fish, to store food for this haul, that the other day a fish hawk swooped down to give me a hungry look!"

I laughed and assured him that we would trim down all too soon, and we would get used to the high altitudes eventually. (Bears and wolves were very resilient and adaptable creatures.)

He mumbled, "Oh, for Greyl's wings right now. She goes from altitude to altitude with never a gasp or puff, and she is lighter than air."

Greyl had been dropping in on us from time to time, giving directions and encouragement. Her commitment and energies on our behalf were truly unbelievable. She was, to us, a winged miracle, and she seemed to prosper under the challenge. We took every chance we could to voice our appreciation and thank her. Neither Lothar nor I could even come to talk about her possible time of departure. That depended on her food supply and her safety—and we knew that was 'her call', not ours.

As we climbed higher up the slopes, the river valley that we were following became deeper, narrower, and harder to navigate. Here, said Greyl, was where we started on the 'goat-ghost' trails to speed up the transit from ridge to high ridge over the range of mountains by trying to avoid the ups and downs of valleys.

Greyl had been scouting these trails whenever she could, subject, of course, to winds and weather. She was grounded by both when conditions were bad, which, at high altitude even in summer, were sudden and violent—as we were to find out.

Greyl was almost always on the wing, apparently exceedingly interested in our mountains. During good days, she would fly over them, returning to the Great Sea to feed and rest at night. Although she seemed to find the routine easy, Lothar and I wondered if she could keep it up. To us, her round-trips were days of arduous travel—to her, they were all in a day's flight.

Because the mountains stretched from west to east, our choice of crossing (from north to south) was at the narrowest part of the range and, although high, where we were to cross, the peaks were not as terrifyingly high as those to the east. Greyl and the 'ghosts' said our routes were passable.

Lothar and I, by this time, had adjusted quite well to the altitude and the exertion. We were congratulating one another on our fitness and survival skills.

When Greyl pointed us to the 'ghost' trails, we found that the going was much harder. Although the 'ghosts' were not there in person to guide us, there was no doubt that they had been there. Where hoof prints and scuffs were not visible, the not-so-subtle aroma of 'ghost' marked the trails! Although the paths were narrow and treacherous, we could follow them without any trouble: Our noses led the way!

By this time, we had lost sight of the Great Inland Sea (although Greyl assured us it was still there) and, guess what: every time we went over a mountain, all that we could see was *another mountain*!

At these high altitudes above timberline, there were scrub vegetation, moss, and other strange survivor-type plants—gray and chewy. Lothar and I found them edible but not tasty. He said if 'ghosts' could live on that stuff, so could a wolf (and a bear)! And we did, although quietly longing for those good old days when we complained about too much fish!

Greyl, with us whenever possible, thought all of that very funny! As our fat quickly melted off of us, we became as lean and wiry as the 'ghosts' (which we never really saw except at a distance).

One particularly clear, calm day—unusual for heights that usually bred constant winds—Lothar and I saw Greyl circling way up above us. It was a nice, comforting feeling, her strong wings protecting us from above. Although we knew that she was no match for an eagle, or some other bird predator, she seemed always to keep them at bay. Another of the mysteries that kept us safe on our mysterious, mystical Journey.

We were traversing a very rocky cut-up mountain surface. Broken masses of outcrops and rock piles were making the going rough. The 'ghost' trails wound us through and among this terrain in directions that we had to trust to bring us safely through a mountain nightmare.

Suddenly, there was Greyl right ahead of us on the ground. "Follow me quickly," she said. "there is an incredibly powerful snow squall bearing down on us, right here and now!" She flapped on, ahead of us.

We sped up without question, rounding a large rock outcrop with a cave-like hollow underneath. "In here…fast!" Greyl shouted.

But almost with that command, the sky turned white, and a violent rush of snow hit us like a thunderbolt, knocking me off my feet. Greyl was slammed against the rock-face under Lothar, who had the fortune to shield her by his own body being bowled over.

In the near white-out, I saw Lothar seize Greyl in his mouth, and still shielding her, crawl into the rock cave, his fur almost pulled off over his head.

I rolled into the cave's mouth, blocking the cave opening with my still-considerable bulk and rump. I could feel the furious wind and ice pellets searing me, even through my thick fur. But I sealed the three of us from what felt like an avalanche of wind, snow, and ice.

Above the frightening roar of the storm, I shouted to Lothar: "Is Greyl all right? Indeed, are you all right?"

"Yes," he shouted back, "she was stunned but not injured—are you all right?"

I had huddled my paws around Lothar to protect him, so he could feel my warmth and movement, although we were both trembling in shock and fear. Yes, we three were safe for the moment, but likely to be buried by the wind-driven snow piling up against me at the cave opening.

We found out later that the unusual calm that we had thought was strange was, indeed, a sign of a violent summer snow squall to come—and it certainly did come! Apparently, Greyl had seen it swooping in from the west and had just moments to dive down to warn us—and note the cave-mouth just ahead of us on the trail. (At that point, it crossed my mind, "Is Greyl a real goose, or some mysterious, winged messenger from my Star?")

My winged messenger shouted just then, from the muffling protection of Lothar's embrace: "These storms come and go fast. Just hang on…it will be over soon!"

Soon took longer than we hoped. We huddled in that dark cave for a seemingly endless time. My bulk had plugged the cave-mouth so effectively that neither snow nor light seeped in. We were warm and protected—and as with most animals in a kind of shock—we slept. Well, at least I slept.

I was awakened by a steady stream of water running down my face from the snow and ice that (along with me) plugged our cave's mouth. There was silence outside; the wind had ceased; the blizzard had ended. If the storm was, indeed, over, and the summer sun had started to burn off the ice and snow, it was time to move.

I tried to roll over and start clawing our way out. But there was no room to roll over; apparently, I was frozen onto the ice/snow plug that had sealed us in. I couldn't move.

I heard Lothar give a yip of surprise when he tried to sit up and hit the low cave ceiling. "Zar," he cried, "can you move at all?"

"I'm frozen on to the ice plug…I can't even wiggle!" I replied, trying not to panic. (My mother's counsel to be a 'thinking' bear with a goal came to mind.)

Lothar crawled carefully out from beneath my grasp and then atop me. He began to claw at the ice above my head where the melt water was coming down. He made enough progress to let in some light, and that speeded up the intrusion of some hope of escape, as well as more water. He dug like a whirlwind, sending sprays of ice and water all over me, himself, and the cave.

I heard a startled "Onk" from Greyl as the showers hit her. Luckily, we had warmed up the atmosphere of our cave so that there was no threat of re-freezing anything again.

I began to think, found a goal, and, then, said to Lothar, "If I can only turn over, I can get all four sets of my claws into the ice-pan."

(I had tremendous claws and believed that I could rip out that frozen cave-stopper in no time.)

"Watch out," I said, "I'm going to give it a try." And I heaved myself over to face the ice-pan, not however, without a very disconcerting ripping sound as my fur and the ice parted company!

"Oops," said Lothar.

"Oh, my," said Greyl.

"Ouch!" said I.

Desperate to get this all over with—and get us all out of this cave—I rose up as far as the low ceiling would permit, hunched my head down as far as I could and rammed my forepaws and shoulders straight through the ice-pan. Well, so much for claws!

My head and forepaws did punch right through that ice-pan! But the force of my effort carried me and the ice (on my shoulders) out into a fair, blue, sunlit afternoon, and onto a slippery, ice-strewn mountain trail, where I slid to a halt, sitting in a snow-drift...backwards.

Lothar and Greyl followed in quick succession, each equally hitting the slippery slope and also landing in the snowdrift—Lothar upside down, paws thrashing in the air—Greyl sailing forth to ride it out like a fairly regal float. They both were laughing uproariously...until they saw me!

There was a long moment of silence, and then they really roared! Lothar tried to regain his footing (to continue to stare and laugh at me, right side up), but he kept slipping down, all four legs splayed out in all directions.

Greyl had her wings out like outriggers, steadying herself as she, too, convulsed with laughter.

I guess I was quite a sight: a great, soggy, dark creature sitting backward in a snowdrift; a giant white ice ruff around my neck, and two paws waving uselessly in the air, a foot's span below my nose and shoulders.

As funny as this whole scene was to my partners, I was quite upset. I had no leverage to stand up or move in any direction. The weight of the ice ruff was completely paralyzing. I just sat there, dejectedly, and pleaded: "Get this blasted thing off me!"

No help was forthcoming from my slipping-sliding companions. I raised my eyes upward, hoping that my Star could help…but what I saw was anything but heavenly. On a rock outcropping over the cave stood two, shaggy, white apparitions…long beards, long faces and with expressions of terror, amazement, disbelief or all of the above!

When I made eye contact with the two apparitions (I now was sure were our 'ghosts') they bolted backwards with bleating, yodeling alarm cries. I let out my own cry of surprise. They disappeared in a spray of ice, and, I guess, I did my own disappearance in a shower of ice.

I had forgotten that I was anchored in a collar of heavy ice. I jumped up; my feet slipped out from under me, and I crashed headfirst onto the ground, shattering that wretched ice collar, and my senses!

When I regained them, Lothar was licking my face in a frantic attempt to bring me back into the world.

I was surrounded by white shards, though, thankfully, not my teeth or my claws—and I was no longer wearing that collar of ice! I felt lighter than air and as free! But, speaking of air—and free—where was Greyl?

Lothar, overjoyed to see me back in life said, "Oh, she flew off in an attempt to reestablish good relations with our 'goats-ghosts', who probably have some very new and vivid accounts of what fiends bears and wolves really are!"

Remembering what that scene must have looked like—and sounded like—I felt sorrow and compassion for the 'ghosts' that I would, probably, never get to thank face-to-face. (However, it must have been a riotously funny show; and even I could laugh about it, being safely out of the starring role, finally!)

* * * *

The summer sun at our high altitude finally did its job and freed up the trails so that we could proceed on our journey.

Luckily, we were on the downside of the mountain range. Apparently, our recent blizzard experience was on the summit of our route, so hardships eased off a little, especially in the food-and-forage department.

Late in the afternoon of the next day, Lothar and I came across a lovely slope of succulents and mountain flowers, which we hungrily rushed to eat and enjoy.

Food had been so scarce lately, even this sparse fodder seemed a feast. We had even begun to enjoy what Lothar had once described as old, second-hand bark scale. In desperation, he had proved that a wolf could manage to survive on something other than meat—and even like it.

We knew that Greyl would locate us and catch up whenever she could, but it was likely to be a few days, because she had to fly back to the Great Inland Sea to find her own food.

Later, this mountain crossing, in retrospect, was recalled as an arduous adventure—made somewhat more pleasant by the spectacular views. The three of us were very fortunate to survive, and that survival was owed to Greyl and her diplomacy with the 'ghosts', which we never got to thank.

Greyl caught up with us a few days later, as we munched our way lower and lower on the mountains. She had fed and rested well during those days, and was eager to explore farther into our next possible route as we came off this most strenuous leg of our Journey.

She reported on her chasing after the frightened 'ghosts', and attempting to calm them from their face-to-face meeting with the fiends: "an upside-down wolf howling in hysterics and a 'fur-mountain' of a bear, wearing some God-awful ice halo around his neck, bellowing for help!"

Greyl's description sent us off into laughter again. We sincerely hoped that she had cleared up the situation and explained our chance encounter (unfortunate-in-its-timing) with the 'ghosts'. She said that she tried. "Although they are very curious, they really have no sense of humor; apparently, they have very little that they find amusing in their hard lives."

They had only replied courteously—though warily—that they appreciated our circumstances and hoped that we were well on our way and that we had found their trails useful!

Then facing me squarely, Greyl added kindly, "By the way, Zar, they are mountain goats, not ghosts. I just haven't had the heart to correct you."

(For once, the joke was on me.)

We certainly did appreciate their trails, their mannerly helpfulness, and their good wishes. We also felt sad that fun and laughter were not much in their lives. But…weren't we grateful that we found them in ours? And joy and wonder too!

So, we ate and laughed and visited our way down the south side of the treacherous mountain barrier, glad to have survived its perils; determinedly on our way on our Journey to who-knows-what, or where.

Book III

The Journey of the Star—West

Chapter 1

The Other Side of the Mountains

Lothar was away on a hunting foray—Greyl was on another aerial scouting trip—and I was alone, content to loll around in a wooded glen with a stream and a pool. The luxury of a bath, and a sunny drying-out rock made this glen a delicious rest stop.

The three of us had decided to stay a while, tending to our respective needs in a very attractive location. Water from the mountains coursed down the south side, as it had on the north side, although the terrain was much different.

The southern foothills seemed to drink up the water before it could go very far into the terrain beyond. Any view of the southern landscape seemed to show a rugged, desert-like place, covered with sparse vegetation and a haze of heat.

The foothills that stretched west and along the mountain range held the best hope for us, water and food being essential to our survival, although Lothar and I had found ourselves very adaptable to anything edible. (Besides, the foothills were cool.)

I luxuriated in the pool—cold as it was from the icy mountain run-off. There were tasty crawfish and amphibians around the shallow, warmer edges, as well as other interesting delights. I found my energies and enthusiasms definitely on the mend. The trials of the mountain barrier had taken a lot out of Lothar and me, although, at the time, we had not paid much attention to the stress. It's usually only at the conclusion of a serious trial that the realization sets in of how hard things really were.

Well, everything was very easy and pleasant right now. I grazed and foraged and swam and napped until I suddenly realized that I was rather alone in all these delights! Where was Lothar? He had been on his own, foraging for over a day. And where was Greyl? Where had her scouting taken her? Was she safe? Would she return?

I had gotten so used to company for so long, my lack of it hit me like a blast of cold air. Bliss turned to concern; concern turned to outright anxiety. I could not 'bear' to continue my incredible Journey without my partners.

Although I had set out many, many seasons ago confident of my mission with only my parents' wise counsel, a Star, and a Star-Stone for companions, I had soon learned that I wanted and, now, needed companions and all that they brought to my life, and that Journey!

I settled onto my sunny drying-out rock platform to watch and listen and worry. In all my adult life I had never employed my Bear Bellow—my full volume roar that bears are capable of using (and that some over-employ). I was a peaceful, low-key animal who had never really had to summon up full-scale anything. (Oh, yes—that ice collar required a large effort, as I recalled.)

I sat on my overlook and gave out a Bear-Bellow to end all Bear-Bellows! At least, I thought so. It rattled me! And as I really tuned up it seemed to rattle a lot of other things, but those were only echoes—no answering wolf-howl, no overhead '*onk*'...just silence after the echoes died away.

Every few moments, I roared again. Still nothing. Even into twilight, there were no familiar voices answering, nothing but my own voice echoing across the hills.

I was very close to panic now, but I did have enough sense left to know that I should stay where Lothar and Greyl had left me. Mounting a search would be futile, so I just sat on my rock and waited—and occasionally bellowed.

By deep darkness, I lay down, head on paws, determined to keep a watch and a listen, praying that the Star would protect them and me, and trying to remember my father words, "...no harm will ever come to you." But worrying is exhausting work: worrying and ROARING are even more so! I fell asleep, only to awaken long into the night.

I was awakened by the Star! Now, how can a silent, cold Star awaken one? Realistically, stars are soundless, but I would swear there was a noise that woke me. It was not a wolf's howl, nor a goose's honk, but a ripple of sound not unlike the chiming of water falling over loose pebbles.

I sat up and looked up. My Star was still where I had left it at dusk—true south. But then, it began to move…still sounding that strange, musical rippling chime. I heard it; I really did!

The Star—ever so slowly—moved from south to almost west: a new bearing, a new direction, but the same old Star…my Star! And it was pointing me on a new course!

My prayers had been answered. The Star was still watching over me—even as I watched it…and I hoped that my companions were safe…and would soon return. I did believe now, that they would be back.

Chapter 2

Borab

I must have dozed off, because, suddenly, the light of dawn began to fade out my Star. It was still in the west where it had moved during the night. Before it disappeared in the daylight, I took a bearing with the Star-Stone on its new position to prove to myself that I was not dreaming about the new heading. I also firmly raked my claws onto the rock's surface to show the new position of our projected course from the old position that I had marked earlier. The difference showed almost a quarter of a circle change from south to west. What an amazing and most miraculous development! I could hardly wait to tell Lothar and Greyl when they returned!

My confidence in the imminent return of my companions was borne out when, after a successful food search and bath, I stretched out on my warm rock. I was drying out, on my back, looking up into a hazy, blue sky, when I saw a familiar silhouette above me—and heard a familiar 'onk', 'onk'!

Greyl spiraled in and plopped down on my stomach, chattering and 'onking' in an enthusiastic reunion. I hugged her carefully (as she disliked rumpled feathers) but with intense emotion and enthusiastic reunion-whines of my own.

"Oh, oh, my dear friend," I cried. "I have some very startling news for you!"

All the while, Greyl was telling me, that she had some news for me!

I sat up, as gently as I could with a flapping, chattering goose on my lap. She seemed as relieved to see me as I was to see her. But my news could wait as I recognized a sense of urgency in her demeanor. I hoped that her news did not include something awful happening to Lothar!

"Lothar?" I asked anxiously.

"Oh, he's fine," Greyl replied. "He's on his way back here as quickly as possible, and he has a surprise for you. But we both were concerned about you."

(Me? Well, everyone was full of surprises today!)

Greyl continued, "Did you hear it last evening?"

"Hear what?"

"There's some huge, horrible beast loose in the foothills! Yesterday—last night—there was a roar, a bellow, as I have never heard before. It must be a lion or a tiger, or some such Huge Savage beast. It came from this area, it echoed all over these mountains. I was so afraid that it was stalking you."

"Me?" I countered, "Me?...As big as I am?"

"Oh, bigger," Greyl hastily added. "You don't make a noise like that. At least, I've never heard you. When I spotted Lothar, he, too, was overwhelmed by the roar, and made a quick return, concerned about you, and fearing what he might encounter on the way!"

(Oops...I suddenly had a notion what, or who, the Huge Savage Beast really was that had made such a roar.)

Now, this situation was too priceless, too overwhelmingly funny to be ignored. I either had to feign deafness (or ignorance) or confess; but both postures were too hilarious to keep to myself. I started to laugh and laugh, and to collapse in hysterics.

"Do you mean this," I gulped, between fits of laughter, and I gave out my best Bear-Bellow, as I had done the previous afternoon and evening.

Greyl rose straight up in the air and gave out a goose-bellow of her own.

"You? You?" she gasped. "You're the Huge Savage Beast?"

"Yes," I replied, humbly, "I'm afraid my roars were simply amplified by the mountains. I am sorry to get the neighborhood upset."

"Why?" Greyl asked, "Why the roaring, were you injured?"

"No...just lonely...I missed you and Lothar...and I was just trying to call you back!"

"Well," she said, "You certainly accomplished that!" Then she broke up in fits of laughter, circling around and around, laughing and 'onking'. "I never knew you had it in you!"

(Actually, I didn't either!)

Then, Lothar arrived on the scene. He leaped up on the rock, then onto my stomach, with cries of his own. "Are you all right? Oh my, oh my...!"

"I'm fine," I replied, hugging him in joy of his safe return. "And I'm afraid I am the Huge Savage Beast that has terrorized our neighborhood. I'm sorry, I was just lonely!"

"A hugely, LOUD lonely," Lothar said, nipping me soundly on the nose. "You scared us half to death...shame on you!"

I apologized again to both Lothar and Greyl (who had settled down, but was still 'onking' and fluffing her feathers in agitation). Then, all three of us broke out again in fits of laughter.

"Well—there goes the neighborhood!" said a very gruff, gravelly voice down below us.

I jumped up in alarm. Lothar, who was now sitting beside me on the rock, also jumped, as startled as was I.

"Oh," he said, "this is my surprise. This is Borab. He is a wild boar, and he is interested in chasing a Star."

I looked down at the strangest-looking animal I had yet seen on this strangest of Journeys. This creature was just as tall as Lothar, but very heavy and solid on short, straight legs. He had no neck. His chunky body just seemed to narrow a little down to a heavy wedge of a head with a long snout. But it was what he was wearing on that snout that really drew attention to him. He sported two, long, curved tusks, on each jaw that curved up and over both jaws—or down and over, depending on how one described the tusks (which were almost indescribable).

He had coarse brownish-black bristles instead of a fur coat, and small, lively black eyes. In short, he was the ugliest animal I had ever seen!

"Isn't he gorgeous?" said Lothar, as if producing a trophy catch. "He is a master at survival in deserts and bad terrain and knows this part of the area well. He is also a master forager for a non-meat killer like you, Zar."

In a hushed aside, Lothar whispered "Say something, you dummy!"

I had been standing there in frozen mid-gawk, actually struck dumb. Luckily, good manners won out over idiocy, and I said weakly, "Welcome Borab, I am Althazar—and this is Greyl." I nodded at the goose circling overhead. She seemed to know the boar because she was laughing and chortling in a contented-bird mode. (Also, I surmised that the situation amused her: to see me so ill at ease.)

Lothar jumped down and stood beside Borab in a sort of sponsoring way. I, too, jumped down so as not to loom over the scene and make it any more uncomfortable.

"This is your Prince?" Borab said to Lothar, "Looks mightily like a bear to me!"

I sat down in front of the boar, because, standing up, I presented a very tall creature. Besides, a sitting posture (for animals) usually showed Peaceful Intent. (I did have the feeling, though, that Borab could easily cut anyone down to size, in many ways, without much effort!)

I said, "In my country, I was considered a Prince because I was the son of a great and wise King. However, I am only a bear…I haven't yet figured out what a Prince really is or what he does. However, one thing I do know: a Prince has good manners and is never to present boorish bad manners. (Oops!) I just did, didn't I—for the second time! Oh, I am making a mess of this. I am sorry!"

With that, Borab gave a snort of amusement and started to laugh. His little eyes twinkled and, I swear one of them winked. (Boorish? Oops!)

"Got to ya, didn't I? My Prince!" He said, chomping those incredible tusks a few clicks. "If you think I'm strange looking, you should see an elephant or rhinoceros, from my home territory. An elephant and rhinoceros defy logical word description, so I shall spare you.

"However, tell me about your Journey of the Star and how such an unlikely crew as a wolf, a bear, and a goose ever got together on a Journey (as Lothar says) into the Unknown to an Unknown Goal, if any, for no other reason except the Journey. And by the way, it is a commanding, princely sound you can make, your Huge Savage Beast Roar! That sort of thing can be very useful."

I guess Borab just looked mean and nasty. I soon discovered that he had a droll and very dry wit, and he was mentally as sharp as his curved tusks.

All four of us went down to the secluded pool and the glade that I had been delighting in for the past few days.

I recounted for Borab the now-old story of the Star, the Star Stone and, what I called, my father's commission to me many seasons ago. At the end of my story, I got the chance to add my surprise.

I told them of the Star music and its movement to the west and of our course's new bearing. No one uttered a sound, though interesting glances were exchanged among Lothar, Greyl, and Borab.

"Honestly, my friends, I am not making this up," I said in earnest. "The Star did sing and it did move. I even marked the old and the new bearings on that rock I have been using as an observation post—go look!"

Greyl spoke finally, "It isn't that we doubt you. It is because after days of surveying the area south of us, Lothar and I had come to the same conclusion, independently…that a Journey south would be impossible because of the dry, hot broken-up desert terrain there. Then we met Borab—a miraculous occurrence in itself—and he, as a lifelong wanderer from the far east, and a good, experienced judge of hardship survival, said: "No way." So you see, we all knew that south was out—but we were committed to your plan, wherever it led us, and we were concerned.

"So, when you told us, all on your own that the Star now led west, I thought (and the others did, too) that another miracle had happened. All our scouting pointed westward as the only way to get around the bad desert conditions. Part of the miracle was Borab coming on the scene at this time. He knows a survival route and truly wants to help."

Lothar and Borab nodded enthusiastically. Again, I was overwhelmed with the way this Journey was working out. I embraced my partners in gratitude and hopefulness and thanked them for working out our future while I was idling around, splashing in my pool and snacking on interesting tidbits.

Then, without delay, we all went splashing and snacking and had a grand party for days before starting out on the next leg of our Journey.

* * * *

Westward now, we kept to the foothills of the mountains. There, the vegetation and streams offered enough food and shelter to keep us fit and happy.

Now, the four of us progressed at a leisurely pace...Greyl still aerial, scouting; Lothar curiously investigating any promising animal trail, and Borab, who as it turned out, was a connoisseur of new foods, constantly diverting to browse, dig, or rip out any intriguing delicacy—and encourage me to try it! Actually, I did sample some tasty (and sometimes appalling to look at) new foods. Borab had a nose for edible stuff, and all of us had a very good and varied diet for a change.

It wasn't long before Lothar and I remarked to each other, "How did we get this far without Borab?"

He was invaluable in his knowledge of the kind of geography we were encountering—its terrain, water and food characteristics—even the animals we might encounter. Although he had never been to this particular area before, his long, nomadic life—moving westward from his origins—had given him a vast amount of experience in various lands and climates.

I doubt if he had any natural enemies. One look at that face, and any predator would certainly back off. He was brazen and absolutely fearless, poking his remarkable snout into the most unlikely places.

My partners were amazingly efficient at keeping our Journey safe and well-nourished. I began to wonder just what I was contributing to the venture. I was the verbal one of the crew—I was the dreamer in charge of our illusive dream; I was the navigator in charge of following the Star, and on occasions, I could be called upon to emit a Bear-Bellow...the Huge, Savage Beast Roar. However, who needed a monstrous sound when we had the real fury in the form of Borab? Well, I was just thankful that the others let me come along with them. I was enjoying the journey...and the company.

Soon after Lothar first presented Borab to me, I asked the two of them just how such an unlikely pair ever got together. Well, it seems Borab had saved Lothar's life!

Lothar had been out in the rocky desert, searching for some food. He had been following a rodent scent, head down, nose to the trail. He had just rounded a big boulder, where he came face to face with the biggest scorpion he had ever seen, in imminent striking mode.

A voice nearby shouted: "Don't move!" A set of sharp hooves descended on the scorpion just as it struck at Lothar's nose.

The scorpion broke up into several parts. Lothar reared back on his haunches—and what turned out to be Borab stood in front of him, gnashing those unusual tusks in a grin or grimace, or 'something'.

Lothar said, still shaking in shock: "Thank you...you saved my life."

"Pleasure indeed...probably wouldn't have killed you, but a sting anywhere on the head could have done a lot of damage. And, by the by, my name is Borab; I am a wild boar—the fearless desert warrior—impervious to stings, bites, weather, other animals, and even insults on my strange looks. Do you want this tasty morsel for lunch?"

Lothar, still shaken, declined politely with a sense of rising nausea. The boar crunched down on the scorpion after separating the stinger.

"Zesty, spicy...delicious!" he remarked.

And so, Lothar met Borab, or visa versa. They chatted as they returned to the foothills out of the desert sun and heat. Borab was intrigued by Lothar's tale of the Journey of the Star and his friend Prince Althazar, and their winged scout, Greyl. By the time darkness had come, the boar asked if he could join the crew, as he had a lot he could contribute. He had always longed for a mission in life outside of being a perennial wanderer—and seeker of exotic and strange foods!

Then the huge roar (of what turned out to be me) vibrated and echoed through the hills. Lothar was alarmed and immediately set off to see if I was safe. Borab asked permission to join up; Lothar agreed, thankful for another strong ally in what could be a hostile scene.

Sometime, the next morning, Greyl spotted Lothar and met Borab. Then she flew off to find me.

So, our seekers of the strange and exotic were augmented by one more—and another natural enemy became a mutual friend. By now, we were not surprised at what—or who—happened on our way to 'somewhere'. We had grown to understand that 'somewhere' was 'today', and the goal was in living that 'today' fully in wonder—and in joy. (And as it seemed, in very diverse company.)

Our way west paralleled a vast, rough desert to our south. Greyl had scouted far into this desert area, as well as into our proposed way that kept us close to water and forage to the north of the desert. She had found two major river systems that broadened out in a southern route to a salty gulf. She had found several other rivers and oasis areas for our western march that would help us all. In fact, Greyl had apparently found enough marshes and watery areas to keep her in good shape on long scouting flights (and us supplied, also).

Oh…for wings. What majesty and mysteries we could share if we only could fly! These hot, arid areas were so very different from our northern homelands of evergreens and meadows; Lothar and I found ourselves a little homesick at first.

But after a few forays into real desert, we discovered an amazing amount of life and beauty. Seasons certainly were very different, but there were astounding cycles of desert flowers and light conditions that contradicted a first impression that deserts were lifeless, unchanging nothingness.

Borab, of course, knew all this and eagerly shared his lifetime experiences, wisdom and discoveries as a desert wanderer. The desert, it seems, could grow on one. To appreciate its subtleties, as well as stark contrasts, one had to slow down and not rush things.

We slowed down and certainly did not rush things. In fact, we rather idled our way west. We never saw any humans; Greyl steered us around the few nomadic humans on our route, for there were few of them in this rather inhospitable area anyway.

We proceeded by night, fed ourselves in the early dawn and dusk of the day, and holed up to rest in the hot times of midday. Thanks to Greyl, we were able to find enough water and forage to keep us in good shape, and we became close to survival experts on some relentless marches between oases.

One early morning, Greyl winged in with the great news that we were headed right for a really outstanding oasis…a large desert spring with marshes and trees and all sorts of greenery, a real paradise of creature comforts for the trail-weary.

This paradise was free of humans or any other threats, and it promised to be a haven of respite for as long as we needed it.

We eagerly started off on Greyl's directions and found our oasis by dusk. By the time we had entered this green paradise, Greyl was already floating around in its good-sized pond, happily grazing on water grains and weeds.

Lothar and I immediately went in for cooling dips while Borab found some accommodating mud to roll around in. We were one very happy crew and slept long and late that night and into the next morning.

For Lothar and me, one of the most cherished aspects of an oasis rest-stop was to soak our feet. Long seasons on our Journey had hardened our pads to endure any surface and distance required of foot travel; but a good soak was a treat beyond description.

He and I had found a half-submerged log in the pond and took turns lying full length on it while our feet enjoyed a time of wet and quiet repose in cool spring water.

Now, before we even explored about, we soaked our feet. Borab, having gone off to find his mud, was probably soaking more than just his feet. A surmise proved right when he appeared, later that day, in a full body-wrap of dried mud.

He joined our own soggy little group where we were dozing on a grassy bank. In his mouth, he carried an unknown 'something', which he carefully laid down before us in the grass. "Lothar, Zar," he said, "mud is powerfully more healing to a trail-weary body than water, why don't you let me show you to a great mud wallow that I've found?"

"What?" replied Lothar, "And come out looking like you?"

Borab countered: "You should be so favored!"

Greyl and I laughed at that one. I said: "He got you there, Lothar old buddy!"

Lothar laughed with us and agreed. Borab was a real droll comic; he was always teasing us about calling ourselves 'princes', so handsome and well-favored. (We didn't, of course, and weren't!)

"What is that revolting black thing that you have brought us?" Lothar asked. "I can't tell if it's something to eat, or it's something I've already eaten!"

"Ah," Borab replied, "it is a delicacy beyond imagination, and it is probably wasted sharing with the likes of you, royal or not."

He snapped off an end of the thing and began crunching with great gusto. He pushed a piece of it towards me, ignoring Lothar. "Come my Prince, show us your true mettle...have a bite. This is really one of the greatest gourmet treats you will ever eat!"

I backed up a bit and with all the princely courtesy I could summon, declined. "Try some Prince Lothar," I said, "show your royal courage!"

Lothar sneezed and also declined.

Greyl entered the scene. "Well, let a feathered commoner try this royal treat. Borab, so far you've always shared very delicious (if not always attractive) treats."

She took a bite of the smaller pieces that Borab had left on the grass. If a goose can register surprise on her face, Greyl did.

"My word, it is not half bad!"

Lothar and I murmured in unison: "What about the other half?"

Greyl laughed, "Try some, my doubting Princes…show us what true sons of Kings are really made of!"

(Lothar said in an aside: "It isn't so much what we're made of as what that stuff is made of!")

Our light-hearted banter and silliness was suddenly cut off by a strange voice from a thicket at the back of the pond.

"You sound and act like royal fools rather than Kings or Princes," the strange voice intruded, forcefully. "I have known and served kings and princes in my day…and you aren't anything like them!" The voice then changed to laughter, which took off the edge.

Chapter 3

Dromed

Borab whirled around, standing his ground and ready to do battle. Lothar jumped backwards and crashed into me. I fell back, also, and slid into the water, sweeping Greyl in under us both. All three of us surfaced, spluttering, to confront and identify the source of this unexpected intrusion into our seemingly peaceful space. (Greyl headed to deep water.)

What we saw (beyond our stout, defiant, desert-warrior Borab) was certainly, one of the most bizarre-looking of the strange animals we had yet seen!

As Lothar and I scrambled back up onto the bank, the strange creature arose—part by part—from the thicket. First, we saw a long head with sloping nose and big loose lips. The head was attached to a long, curved neck, and if the neck was downward-curved like a valley, the white body it was attached to stood up like a tall, humpy hill. This valley and hill appearance was further exaggerated by the creature rising rump first!

When finally unfolded, the creature stood way above me (even when I was fully unfolded) on long knobby legs, and its expression of disdain and haughtiness was even more distracting than its strange looks! (It was a natural look for his species, I found out later.)

Well, as leader for the 'royal fools', I felt I should make courteous niceties, even though we were almost speechless in surprise.

"Greetings!" I said, hoping to drip goodwill (rather than just water from my soggy fur). "I am Althazar; this is Lothar; the tusked one in front of us is Borab, and the goose in the pond is Greyl." (I purposely left off any embarrassing titles to explain.) "We are on a Journey of the Star—to a destination and purpose yet to be revealed—if indeed it ever will be. If that doesn't make a lot of sense, it is because it just doesn't." (I trailed off lamely, as I realized I wasn't exactly doing this right) then added in last resort, "But our intent is entirely Peaceful!"

The awkward-looking creature in front of us surveyed our scene in long silence from beneath fringed, large, long-lashed eyes. (Indeed, those were the most beautiful and compelling aspects of his entire make-up.)

Borab said, breaking the spell: "That is a camel, a white camel; I have encountered camels before on my desert wanderings."

The camel said then, "Although fairly harmless and very ungainly looking, and considered stupid, stubborn, lazy, and unlovable, I, as a camel, am very old and very wise and unfortunately, very inclined to be unkindly judgmental. But I am not stupid and unlovable, although I am 'indescribable'.

"My name is Dromed, and I have called this oasis home for many seasons. You are welcome; though I was quite surprised by your sudden appearance here!"

Borab said, as an aside to Lothar and me, "See? It's not only an elephant or a rhinoceros that I could not describe in words for you! A camel, too, would be indescribable! Ha!"

"Ha! Indeed," said the camel Dromed, who had heard our exchange.

I felt that we had gone as far as we could with the 'ha's'. It was time for action to back up my words.

I sat down, and Lothar did likewise. Borab also gave up his menacing posture: raising his head and lowering his rump. Sitting, for a boar, was less of a statement of Peaceful Intent than a comical position that usually produced laughter all around and almost always broke up any hostile situation.

This time was no exception! We laughed and so did Dromed and when he sat down, we all laughed even harder, including Greyl, as she paddled ashore to join our merriness. (A sense of humor had rescued us once more!)

We began to share histories and personal experiences, and we became acquainted rather quickly and easily, once our obvious differences and mistrust were overcome.

It was Borab who really broke down the barriers by explaining that white camels (like Dromed) were especially treasured by human princes, because they were very rare and set apart, befitting high human status. Dromed was one of those special riding camels, wasn't he?

Dromed was obviously pleased to be recognized as special, but demurred that his great age had diminished his unusual true white suit with gray. He said, "Yes,

I carried a king once, on a long journey to the west. (A long journey much like yours, perhaps?)"

He inquired about my reference to the Journey of the Star. He listened in growing interest and wonder as I told about my quest, the start of my Journey, and the subsequent joining up with Lothar, Greyl, and Borab that had become 'our' Journey.

We recounted our adventures at length. Dromed seemed genuinely engaged and also genuinely amused at our antics and storytelling. He said he had been very much alone at this oasis for a long, long time and was very grateful for conversation and company—a feeling that he had not recognized until now—when he found himself in pleasant companionship, enjoying exchange of other experiences than his own, of which he was a little weary.

We talked together well into the evening. By that time, Dromed had begun his own story—and that would take us through the night and into the next day. Actually, well into the rest of our lives!

It was a story of mystery and wonder that set our ruffs up in awe and excitement. All four of us wondered at the mystic movement of fate that brought us together, at this time, with this stranger, this ghostly white camel, this wise unlikely creature of destiny.

Indeed, I began to wonder and to believe, we were all strangers of destiny—mysteriously and mystically now friends and companions—come together, on what would turn out to be another Journey of the Star.

So, Dromed told us his story and a new direction in our lives opened.

CHAPTER 4

OF CAMELS AND KINGS

Dromed was born into and grew up in the household stables of a king. He was part of the riding-camels' elite, as opposed to the baggage-camels' herd. That differentiation, as well as his unique white coat, was enough to single him out as his King's own special camel. When the King went out locally, he rode a magnificent white horse; when he took long desert trips, he chose to ride a special white camel, which, (when mature and trained), was Dromed.

By the time an ordinary camel is weaned and ready to be really domesticated, its mother has tried to impress upon it the finer rules of camel-hood: always groan and moan at the slightest suggestion of work: that is anything that is to be loaded on its back, or anything that even suggests moving from its present position of rest and indolence. Camels must always appear to be overworked, overloaded, and under-appreciated; they must appear haughty, miserable, grumpy, and evil-tempered. Most of them did all that very well.

Dromed began his riding-camel training before he was thoroughly imprinted with all these rules, and therefore, he was happy, gentle, and well-mannered.

For this attitude, he was ostracized by his peers—a life of aloneness that rather suited him (as he didn't really like or belong with camels) and that loner-style prepared him for the life he now lived, and had lived for so long. Although, he confessed he dearly missed his King.

Dromed's King was not so much a ruler over many lands and humans as he was a very revered Wise Man. He had large houses and possessions and was very rich, but mostly he was a mystical, spiritual sage who was very knowledgeable about potions and prophecies, and especially about things past and things to come, as written in the stars. He and his fellow kings counseled together about things more than earthly...things that Dromed did not really understand.

This King, this Wise Man, was a very gentle and kindly man, beloved by all his people and servants. He was especially fond of his stable of horses and camels. In exchange, his white horse and white camel were very favored. They all wore a distinctive royal mark, or brand.

Although Dromed could understand much of human speech, he found that humans could not—or chose not to return the favor. It was a great mystery to all the domestic animals that he knew, why humans, who were very intelligent, thinking creatures, could not really communicate with animals.

It might have been that humans thought animals were of lesser worth than they—or that animals were sub-human and therefore could not speak or think or feel. But all that Dromed knew of his King seemed not to bear out that inequality, because his King was so loving, kind, and thoughtful.

(This inability to comprehend or include animals in their 'life respect' was to puzzle all of us all our lives, as we—Lothar, Greyl, Borab, and I—proceeded on our Journey and moved closer into the company and ideas of humans.)

About this time in Dromed's story, the four of us broke in with our own mysteries. That is, what did Dromed mean when he spoke of things like horses, houses, possessions, being rich? He had mentioned cities, gardens, stables and servants. All these words were familiar to Dromed but not to us, and much of the day was spent in defining his terms.

We had a hard time understanding houses and cities, riches and possessions; but above all, we had a very hard time visualizing men and women, and how they were clothed, how they lived, how they looked, and did they think Ideas? We thought it very funny (and laughed heartily) when Dromed explained that you could tell the males from the females because one had long beards in front and the other had long manes in back! And their young had large heads but neither beards nor manes until older. (And yes, they spent a good deal of time arguing about Ideas!)

Dromed really was the most patient of teachers. He never criticized us, nor scolded us when our incomprehension bordered on the crazy, and we would laugh and clown around with descriptions and terms. We were boisterous but interested students, though definitely on the skeptical side when trying to understand what—for us as creatures of the wild—sounded bizarre and unimaginable. It certainly is as hard for an animal of the wild to go domestic as the other way around, maybe harder. Although, Dromed had been domestic and now was wild and seemed to have adjusted quite well.

So, we asked, if you liked your work, and loved your King, why are you up here in this remote oasis, living in the wild, far from your domestic roots?

"Ah," replied Dromed, with a faraway look in his eyes, "That is the story of the Kings and their Star…"

Dromed explained that his story of the Kings and their Star began when he was in his young prime as a riding-camel—many, many years ago. (Of course, he had to explain the term 'year' to us as a measure of time: a cycle of four seasons.)

He was a very old camel when he met us, wise and experienced; but when the Kings' Star Journey began for him, he was young, vigorous, full of life, curious wonder, and very proud to be a Royal Camel and to wear the mark.

He explained that his experience and understanding of the Star and the Kings came through personal involvement (the 'action' phase) and through overheard conversations of the King and his friends (the 'Idea' phase). He had heard what he called 'stable gossip', that is, the chatter of other animals, or servants, and grooms about their mission, the Star expedition.

It seems that one day Dromed's King noticed a special happening in the heavens, a convergence, a coming together of stars at a particular time in history, that signified a very unusual, unique occurrence: the birth of a King, (most unlike the Kings he knew) in a small country to the west called Judea. This King-to-be-born was to be known as the King of the Jews (at that point Dromed had to digress once again to explain 'Judea' and 'Jews') and this new king was to be like no other before him in history: a King over men's hearts and souls *not* lands.

Dromed's King and his fellow astronomer Kings met together to discuss this coming event. They affirmed its significance in their religion (one of star portents) and agreed that they should all mount an expedition to go west to Judea, by a Great Sea called Mare Nostrum, to pay homage to this baby King, this King of hearts and souls.

A great train of camels and baggage and gifts were organized. The Kings and many servants set out to follow the Great Star, which the Kings could see, going before them, leading them to the west.

Dromed—as his King's camel—led the way. The train marched by night and rested in tents during the heat of the day. As this was a vast desert that they were crossing, the train had to carry food and water with them, counting on few oases along the way to rest and refuel.

As camels could go for days without water, they were, of course, the carriers of necessity. Dromed was honored to be the top-ranking camel of all the train, which meant that he was posted right next to his King's tent where he could overhear the discussions that the Kings exchanged. And although Dromed understood much of kingly language, he couldn't always understand what it all actually meant, because so much of the words were related to the Star.

(Of course, we four listeners couldn't understand much of Dromed's language and had to interrupt him over and over again to explain. Even then, we didn't fully comprehend all his explanations! I commented that we were a lot luckier on our Journey of the Star because there were few word-explanations needed, as we didn't understand any of our expedition anyway! The four of us—Lothar, Greyl, Borab, and I—laughed at that extreme comment, because we had long since discovered that our Journey was our goal. But Dromed, a bit puzzled by our explanation, understood that his Journey was focused on a specific goal (as we were learning).

Dromed's caravan took routes across the desert that avoided towns, cities, or conventional roads. Because no matter how his Kings looked, dressed in desert clothing like all caravan travelers—there was really no disguising a certain look of riches. Of course, many camels and such a rich appearance was a temptation to nomad robbers.

Their Star Journey took quite a time, and the usual harshness of the desert—heat, sandstorms and road perils—were hard on the Kings. Relief came in the form of an oasis here and there, but this harsh existence was the only life that camels knew. Their special adaptations (that make them strange to look at, awkward, splay-footed and humpy) were what made them unequalled desert transportation.

Dromed explained that besides the camel-handlers, grooms and servants, there were well-armed warriors that accompanied the Kings as guards.

Civilization—as he called it—only existed in towns and cities where there was some sort of civil law. Out in the desert, there was only the law of survival and predation.

(Believe me, all this was hard for us to comprehend, because we four wild animals could not picture what Dromed's words portrayed; such words as law, civilization, warriors, grooms, baggage, tents were unknown to us.)

Thanks to Dromed's patience as a teacher, we learned many new and strange things about the world, and about Dromed's lack of sympathy with camels as a species. "A bunch of gripers and whiners," he said, "A sorry lot, that had no appreciation for the meaning of their Journey or even their place in this momentous event!"

Dromed became so irritated at the grumbling of his fellow camels that he made a special effort to clue them into their special Journey. He would join them when the caravan rested from the heat of the day and try to improve their 'attitude', as he called it. When his camel herd mumbled about their harsh treatment and heavy burdens, Dromed asked them if they had ever displayed any affection or enthusiasm to their handlers? "Of course not," was the unanimous reply.

"Well," replied Dromed, "you might try giving them that which you would like to receive!"

"Like what?" was the disdainful retort.

"Like respect, gentleness, thoughtfulness, courtesy...like all the attitudes that you think you deserve, but don't receive—give what *you'd* like to get!"

Well, that dialogue with his grumpy group of brother camels didn't go anywhere, so Dromed went back to his appointed station by his King's tent and decided to sing softly to himself about all the good things that he received and saw and heard, and learned from listening to the Kings.

He sang about the desert and the blazing sun; he sang about the cold nights and the carpet of bright stars over his head. But especially, he sang about this special Star Journey and its special meaning of a birth of a King, for whom he and his camel brothers—and his Kings—were bringing honor and adoration.

Then a strange thing happened: one by one the other camels would creep softly to Dromed and settle around him to listen to the songs. And some of them began to sing with him—and their hostile-camel 'attitude' began to soften.

This singing went on throughout the whole long Journey, and even the Kings seemed to hear it. They remarked in awe, that the 'Song of the Camels' was a very strange and special occurrence and was truly a mystical and Holy thing!

CHAPTER 5

THE GIFTS OF THE MAGI

The end of Dromed's journey took the caravan through more and more populated lands until one day it came to the outskirts of a great city. The caravan halted near a spring in an olive grove, and made preparations to enter the city the next day.

That night, the blazing star that they followed seemed almost overhead; at least, there was a bright glow in the sky. So, was this the place the Kings had sought? No, their destination was farther south.

Dromed overheard their conversation from their tents. The next day the Kings would enter the great city—the capital of this land of Judea—and make a courtesy call on the ruler of the land, both to introduce themselves and their mission and to get directions to the birthplace of the new King that they sought.

The strangest part of the Kings' Star Journey was that only they—the Wise Men, the Magi (the Kings)—seemed to see the Star! The animals (in this case, the camels) never really saw a single blazing star but affirmed to each other that the heavens were teeming with stars. But then, they were only beasts; and a heaven full of stars, or any one star more prominent than any other, seemed to be the construction of the mind of whomever made the judgment. All beings saw things differently.

Dromed and the other camels were led by their Kings, and if their masters said that they all were following a Blazing Star, then they were: they followed, Kings and camels.

(At this point in Dromed's story, I broke in and asked him, point-blank, if his Star Journey was real, or was it all in the minds of his Kings? Dromed said that he believed that the Star only appeared to his Kings, and that further questions to other animals, that they encountered later, confirmed this belief. The Star was only seen and interpreted by the Kings and if any others believed that they saw it, it was revealed only to *humans* at that time.

'Humans'...Dromed used a word that we *thought* we understood. Could it be that the description that Dromed gave us earlier of 'men' and 'women' was really that of those creatures that we had previously seen (hind-leg walking), that we called 'exotics'? After much animated discussion, and frustration all around, we all finally agreed, "Yes." 'Men' and 'women' are *humans*!

So what about us? I asked, we animals who now followed a Star—was it real or only in 'believing minds', so to speak?

Dromed asked me; did I see my Star? I replied, "Of course, why else would I...we...make this journey?")

* * * *

Dromed continued, suggesting that if the first appearance, or revelation, of the Star was to humans, the second revelation might be to animals and all other creatures. That idea really hit the four of us like a shock wave! Did it mean, then, that I, Althazar, an animal, a Bear, could see and follow a Star like Dromed's Kings of long ago? And Lothar, Greyl and Borab, too?

"Well," continued Dromed, "Let me continue, and maybe you will find your own answers!"

So, Dromed went on with his story, even as Lothar, Greyl, Borab, and I exchanged puzzled and questioning looks. Wow!

* * * *

It was barely light the next morning when the grooms began to prepare Dromed and the other Kings' riding-camels for their entrance into the great city. The ceremonial saddles and bridles were brought out of the baggage containers and readied for the morning procession.

The trappings were of great beauty and brilliant colors; the saddle cloths of intricate oriental designs were edged in scarlet and gold; the bridles and reins were heavy with embroidery of the same, and also edged in small, golden bells. A sound like wind-chimes echoed with every movement.

When fully equipped, the musical camels were dazzling. Dromed was always overjoyed to wear his King's livery, and never quite got enough time to show off his regal deportment—in full dress, as it were.

Of course, the full-dress events were not at all an everyday experience, so he and his fellow camels made the best of it, putting on all the grace and style that a camel could achieve for the occasion.

When the Kings came out to mount and begin their ride, they were also in full-dress regalia—startling and stunning in the richness of their robes' colors and textures. This all made the long effort almost worth the journey's time and hardships. The camels believed this procession was the great event that they had come for!

"Not so," whispered Dromed. This was only the first act of the event. It was a newborn baby that they sought, not the old King of Judea that their Kings were meeting this morning. "Too bad," whispered back his fellow camels. "This show would delight the eyes of any young one. Why waste it on an old man?"

When Dromed's King came to the crouching Dromed, he stroked his camel's cheek and cupped his nearest ear, whispering: "Isn't this the greatest? You know, most of being a King is in playing a 'Royal Act'. Most of royalty is simply putting on a good show and acting as if we deserve it…or know what we're doing. But isn't it fun?"

He chuckled and mounted onto Dromed's tall, gold-edged saddle, clucking for him to rise.

Dromed stood up, turned his head to meet his King's eyes…and he swore that his King winked!

They strode off to the city. The Kings and several guards and retainers entered the gates to the accompaniment of shouts and cheers, as mobs of city folk clustered around them to enjoy the parade. Any break in their boring lives, especially such a colorful, jingling parade, made for an excuse to gather and cheer. Who didn't enjoy a parade?

(Of course, here we broke into Dromed's narrative to ask about all the new words—saddles, bridles, bells, and what was a *parade*?)

Dromed patiently explained, then continued his story (referring, as usual, to himself by his name):

Dromed led the parade, following a mob of city folk escorting the procession to the palace of their King, but hardly making room for the camels to pass through the narrow streets. It was a near riot, but a joyous one, and all the hands that reached out and the cheers were friendly and welcoming. It was one very proud moment for Dromed. He carried himself and his King with great style and elegance of movement, careful of his feet and legs to avoid squashing any men or women, but especially careful of the children whose mothers held them up to see and touch the Kings.

It was an anticlimax when they reached the palace and entered the gates that closed to shut off the crowd and noise.

The camels knelt and the Kings dismounted to enter the palace, escorted by courtiers. The camels were led to a shady courtyard and given food and water while their masters were elsewhere. Dromed especially treasured the figs and dates that were offered. With their mouths otherwise occupied, the camels did little chatting, but they all knew that there would be much to tell and retell when they returned to camp and informed the baggage-camels about that great morning. Of course, they, the camels, would be the center of all the attention for the parade—and the retelling! What a shallow and vain group they were, these camels, thought Dromed, but he suddenly realized that he too, wanted to tell someone—and revel in 'The Show'!

Great ceremonial moments were all too few, but maybe a great dazzling parade would be put on for the baby King, and Dromed could again lead the show!

The ride back to the camp in the olive grove outside the city walls was not quite as tumultuous as the parade going in; but there was still an enthusiastic crowd to line the streets to shout and stare.

Dromed did his best to step out in elegance and style, all the while hoping to hear some of the conversation of the Kings about what went on in their palace interview. The Kings, however, didn't speak—or couldn't—above the noise of the crowd. So, it was much later, when the glorious harnesses, regalia and furnishings were put away, and everyone had settled down for the night, that Dromed sneaked up close to his King's tent and overheard all the post-event conversations of the Kings.

It seemed that his Kings had been rather unimpressed by the King of Judea, and they referred to him as a 'pompous little sneak' or something like that. None of the Kings saw or felt anything in the man that made for trust or respect, despite the ornate show of their audience and refreshments that the King of Judea lavished on them.

At the King of Judea's statement that he was respectfully awaiting news of the young King's birth so that he could go and honor him, Dromed's Kings, now safely out of the audience, snorted in derision. They wouldn't trust him or his henchmen to do any good for the baby, and would not consider giving away any time or place of the birth. "That pompous so-and-so is a crafty, cunning idiot—and dangerous!"

The rest of the conversation was spent in making plans for the following days and in devising ways to avoid the King of Judea's spies, which they knew would be tailing them.

The next day, the whole caravan packed up and made a wide sweep around and away from the city, first east to confuse any spies, then a long sweep to the south, then west, where the Star had appeared during the previous night.

It was a long ride around the city, but Dromed's caravan finally found the open country, away from settlements and villages. If anyone was tailing them, it was open enough to see who and where they were. So, they rode one day and one night in their long way around, sending their most skilled scout back to see if the spies were still on their trail.

When Dromed's caravan finally set up camp for the next night's rest, his King told the scout to go back, find their trailing spies and when it was feasible—such as just before dawn—quietly round up the spies' camels and take them to the nearest village and leave them. This would put the spies in the sad predicament of having to tail the caravan on foot, which would soon dampen anyone's enthusiasm for following mounted adversaries.

The plan worked beautifully, and the scout never again saw anyone on the caravan's tail. The Kings and the caravan thought the entire episode vastly amusing, and stable gossip had it that one of the Kings had said heartily:

"Well, that should stop the slimy little weasel and his treacherous little game!" (He meant the King of Judea, of course!)

That night the Kings were exceptionally excited because the Star seemed to be hovering over a small village over the nearest hills. Everyone, including the camels, thanks to Dromed's ballads, was eager to finish the search for the baby King, and even the camels saw a glow in the sky that night.

A camp was set up in a valley near the village. The Kings went to the baggage train and filled their saddlebags with special gifts that they had brought with them.

Dromed assumed that the ceremonial harnesses and all would be put on for this greatest of events. For sure, this was what the whole long Star Journey was about!

But the Kings did not change into their ceremonial robes, and their camels were not dressed the way they thought they should be. Only the small harness bells that they wore on their everyday trail bridles were in evidence, and that seemed a small gesture, indeed, for such an occasion.

Dromed could only guess that the Kings thought discretion in honoring the baby was safer than royal display. Dromed was mightily disappointed, because he believed that if he were a baby, bright colors, and golden bells would be far more fun than what the Kings loaded in their saddle bags. Whatever was in those saddlebags was very smelly and Dromed sneezed when his King put the load on him.

The Kings mounted their camels and went on alone to the village. Only the muffled jingle of bridle bells and the soft scuff of camel feet sounded in the night. A dog barked from some distance, and a cock crowed, nearby. These were the only sounds to be heard as the Kings rode slowly by the dark houses of the little village.

They stopped by a particular house where a soft, glowing light illuminated the otherwise darkened street. The muffled sound of a baby crying came to them.

Dromed's King dismounted and walked to the entrance of the little house; he quietly tapped on the door. The door was opened ever so slightly and a man's voice asked, "Who is there?" in a language that Dromed had never heard before.

But Dromed's King—a very wise and learned man—replied in the strange language. Whatever he said was immediately welcomed, because the door opened fully, and an old man came out. He beckoned to the Kings to dismount and to enter. They did, taking the saddlebags with them.

Upon the man's insistence they handed the bridles over. The man departed to walk the camels around the back of the house, where he tied Dromed and his fellows to a hay crib in a shed next to a donkey and a milk-cow. ("Oh dear"...thought Dromed, "hay...no figs? No dates?")

The radiance that surrounded the little house extended to the animal shed so that Dromed and his fellows could see fairly well; but they did not see the rooster until it let go with a loud crowing almost next to them.

The camels jerked their heads up at the blast of sound in their ears, but the shed's ceiling was low, and their heads were very tall, and all of them cracked their heads on the ceiling planks!

At the cracks and subsequent cries of the stunned camels, the donkey spoke sharply: "Now see what you've done, you silly bird! It's not near dawn and you crow loudly enough to wake the town. Now, you've startled these tall beasts into hurting their heads!" The donkey gave a sharp kick to the wall on which the rooster sat. The bird scrunched down and gave a few peevish clucks, then fell silent.

"I apologize on behalf of this bird here who sounded off without a thought for the nerves of his companions. My name is Solomon and I welcome you, belatedly."

In the now quiet shed, Dromed and his fellows murmured their introductions as courteously as they could, still slightly dizzy from bumped top-knots.

Dromed spoke: "Do you know if that is a newborn baby King in there with our masters? We camels have come from very far in distance and time to pay him homage. Now, we seem to be stuck back here, well out of 'the action', so to speak."

The donkey, Solomon, replied, "Well there is surely a baby in the house. But he isn't as newborn as he was…that is. I carried his mother to a town nearby a time ago where she birthed the little one in a 'kind of stable', a cave, really. As far as for his being a king, I would find it hard to see that in him or his parents. They are simple, country folk with me, as their only possession.

"It was an event, though, that birthing. At first, there were only some stable animals in the cave, and me, of course. But, then a bunch of shepherds appeared—a noisy, smelly bunch, yet full of great joy and admiration.

"But they all fell silent in awe when they saw the little fellow and his young mother and the kindly older father.

"There was definitely a special aura about the scene. A touch of the Holy, I'd say. But then, there is always a touch of the Holy about new life birthed, in any form, don't you think? A birth is always a Holy thing."

Dromed nodded; but he had never really thought about it in that way before. The birth of a special King had seemed almost other-worldly in his imagination, so he didn't quite want to admit its reality in an ordinary little crying human surrounded by ordinary country folk and stable animals. He wondered how his King saw all of this. To Dromed, a Royal Camel, this all seemed a little common, a little dingy. He wondered if his King and all the Kings weren't a bit out of their class?

Solomon seemed to be extremely chatty. Probably because he was so confined to the company of a crazy rooster, that kept sounding off at regular intervals, and a stolid milk-cow that never uttered a word, but just chomped away on her hay during all the conversation.

"Can't help it," the rooster said between crowing intervals. "It's a new day, a new world, a new life! Everybody SING! Welcome, welcome the wonders of this day!"

"Oh, God," thought Dromed. "This isn't the way I thought it would be. I don't see the child. I don't see our Kings. I don't see any glorious event! I can't even sing, or squeak, to welcome the day that this crazy rooster sees! Oh dear…oh dear, oh, oh, oh!"

Daylight had definitely come before the Kings themselves came to the shed to collect the camels. Dromed bade Solomon goodbye and thanked him for his information and his courteous welcome. But, he ignored the rooster and the cow, because he couldn't get a word in edgewise with the former, and the latter seemed oblivious to any of the goings on.

The Kings mounted in silence. They turned the camels in the direction of their camp. The old man stood in the doorway of the little house. Dromed noticed a glow around the man even in the daylight. He puzzled about this.

Dromed could see through the doorway, a shimmering light illuminating the inner room of the house. For an instant, Dromed's eyes met that of a young woman, holding a baby. She was rocking and singing to the baby. There on the floor, beside them, Dromed could see an array of colorful boxes and gold treasures. Dromed knew these were the gifts of his Kings. But what would these simple people ever do with such treasures? Dromed thought that surely another donkey, a cart, or even hearty wool robes, or food, would have served the little family better!

But Dromed was just an animal, and his animal imagination could not fully take in Star-Portents and Royal Holy Births in a stable. As the Kings' group departed, Dromed sadly realized he had missed wearing his ceremonial livery; and no bells had jingled for the little King.

Perhaps, in his singing, the rooster really gave the better gift on this morn!

Chapter 6

The Aftermath

Dromed suddenly stopped recounting his Star Journey story. There was a sad remoteness in his eyes and a feeling of distress that reached out to us all.

Lothar, Greyl, Borab, and I exchanged meaningful glances, and I said to Dromed, "What happened, my friend?"

He replied, slowly, hesitantly: "I haven't had occasion in all these years to retell my story. I hadn't realized how very 'over' it all was, and how it affected me then, and even now!"

"Well," I countered, "You did get from 'there' to 'here' somehow, at some time. But if the story is too much for you at this moment, we will not press for it. We will just thank you for such an epic story, and be grateful for your presence here, now. Will you join us for our Journey of the Star into the Great Unknown?"

I let it hang there: our invitation.

Dromed nodded. "It is all right. I will tell the conclusion of my Star Journey...and maybe you all will find something that will assist you in your's. There was great meaning in my experiences, but it has taken me a long time to recognize—or to process—that meaning."

Dromed began again.

After the Kings returned to their camp, they gave the orders to pack up for an immediate exit from Judea. The urgency of this move puzzled everyone—man and beast—but, of course, they all obeyed quickly.

The caravan left by an altogether different route than it had used to enter this land. It went north, paralleling the coast of the Mare Nostrum and found itself in a land of rather impressive mountains and valleys, forested with giant cedar trees. The caravan made a turn to the east when far enough out of range of the King of Judea's spies.

Dromed finally found out the reason for their hasty exit, when he overheard the Kings talking about finding the baby King. It seems that during their visit, after giving their gifts and discussing their recent audience with the King of Judea, Dromed's Kings discovered that the old man, the husband of the young mother, had just had a vivid, startling dream. It warned him to leave the country; to go south into another land called Egypt; and to settle there until the King of Judea was dead. The family intended to start the next day.

Dromed's Kings were also startled by the man's dream, because they had experienced the same warning in their recent dreams—to leave Judea right away and to avoid anyone who could report to the King where, and who, the young child was that was born to be a new King of the Jews. But their dreams ordered Dromed's Kings to go *north* before they turned east and returned to their own lands. Apparently, the King of Judea was an enemy and viewed the baby as a threat to his own political power. The Kings had felt *that* all along.

The timing of the dreams and the visit of Dromed's Kings seemed mystically providential. But all of the men in this story were tuned to portents or revelations, and so their responses were immediate and unquestioned.

Dromed did not relate the details, nor the mystical aspects of his overheard conversations, to any of the other camels. He felt the gravity of the whole experience and didn't understand the political or religious implications, but he felt, intuitively, that the Star and the baby King were a very big 'something'. He still got the shivers and shakes whenever he brought everything back to his mind to ponder what it all meant.

The biggest puzzlement to Dromed was one particular sentence, spoken by Dromed's King: he referred to the little baby as 'the Prince of Peace'. A mighty awesome title or role for such a wee one, thought Dromed, but then, for all his knowledge of the strange, hostile antics of the human race that he had heard or seen, Dromed believed that some kind of instrument of peace was vitally and urgently needed!

Dromed just hoped the world would let the little one grow up a bit before that mantle was laid on him!

(Again Dromed stopped his story, and again we didn't hurry him, but we still were thirsting to hear how he came to be at this oasis, and as he had intimated, how and why he had spent long years away from his beloved King and his post as a Royal Camel.)

It seems that somewhere between the Cedar Mountains and their homeland, Dromed became ill and could no longer fill his role as his King's lead camel. His saddle and gear were transferred to a back-up camel, and his King led him slowly for as long as he could keep up. The other Kings and the rest of the caravan were very concerned and patient. Dromed had become a mentor to the other camels, and his singing had brought beauty and meaning into lives that were otherwise very dull and empty.

For a few days, he and his King lagged behind the main caravan, still in sight. Every step for Dromed was painful; he could hardly breathe, and a constant cough racked him.

When they finally dragged into a small oasis, Dromed collapsed. His King brought him food and water, but he was unable to manage them, and lay full length in some shade, with his head in his King's lap.

The King was so distressed at Dromed's condition that they spent several days resting and waiting for improvement. Finally, the King realized that Dromed had to be left behind. None of the herbs and medicines that the King and the others had tried to heal Dromed had worked.

Just before he slipped into a coma, Dromed's King held him and assured him that he was the best and most beautiful camel in the world. His King told him that he would recover, and he would be able to follow the caravan's trail when he was well. Then he whispered: "Dromed, you will always be my lead camel—in my heart!"

The King left the oasis to rejoin the caravan, camped nearby. Dromed's last sight before he slipped into unconsciousness was of his beloved King's face, streaming with tears and looking back at him as he strode away.

Dromed said that he had no idea how long he lay there at that oasis. But eventually, he awoke, and though very weak, could manage to get up and drink from the spring. He found a little forage to eat. Time passed and eventually Dromed came back to life, but, by then, any tracks of his caravan had long since disappeared in drifting sand.

He wandered and searched, wandered and searched for what must have been years. He met no one and just moved from oasis to oasis until he finally admitted that the life he knew and loved was over for him. Yet, he had his glorious memories: of a gentle and kindly Wise Man and the promise of a new world in a tiny man-child Prince of Peace. It was about as much as any camel could dream of—and he still could dream, couldn't he?

Book IV

The End of the Journey

Chapter 1

One More for Our Road

There was no question that Dromed was to join us. His many lonely years of wandering had left him vulnerable to depression and aimlessness. We all read in his demeanor a yearning to belong and enjoy the journey again, any journey. It was not hard to persuade him to add his wisdom and desert savvy to our crew—and to laugh and dream again, and to enjoy amiable banter and conversation.

Dromed, obviously, was one of those rare, special few of us animals who could reason and understand Ideas—and we needed him!

We spent a goodly amount of days at Dromed's oasis. It was stocked with forage and water and shade—all the necessities for rest and relaxation: grain and a pond for Greyl, rodents and amphibians for Lothar; strange exotic roots and tubers for Borab (as well as his beloved mud) and all the above for me.

One day, I noticed Dromed gazing hungrily at some palm trees. The sadness of his expression touched my heart, and I went up to him to comfort him however I could. "Is there anything I can do for you, old lad?"

He replied, still studying the palm trees, "Zar...do you climb trees?"

That was the last thing I would have thought he would ask; I was quite taken back.

"Why yes," I said. "Bears are notorious tree climbers. The only trouble I might have is in my present heavy size, I might weigh the tree down."

"Not a bad idea...that," said Dromed, "have any of you ever tasted DATES? They are heaven-on-earth to me. But I have lived here for unknown years with those enticing pieces of heaven hanging just out of my reach. Sometimes a bunch would fall, but they would be almost inedible by the time they fell on their own. I drool just looking at them!"

By this time, our other three partners had gathered to contemplate the date palms. Greyl flew up and dislodged a few. There were enough for each of us to try one, Dromed included.

"My goodness," we all said, practically in unison, "they are heavenly!"

Greyl tried to tear off some more but she called down and said, "Zar...this is really a job for brute force. Come on up!"

"Thanks for the compliment, the brute says," quipped Lothar. "He's on his way. Now, Prince Brute, try not to bring the whole tree down...remember your last good deed with a tree rescue!"

I curled a lip at Lothar and attacked the tree trunk with gusto. Greyl was waiting for me at the top just above the clusters of dates. I ripped off every cluster I could find. The whoops of joy that I heard down below were reward indeed.

I backed down carefully and was awarded a clump of my own. Dromed was practically weeping tears of joy as he munched.

Lothar asked, "Do you crunch the seed or do you spit it out?"

Dromed turned to face the pool nearby, curled his lips and tongue in a spiral and shot a pit far out into the water!

We all were delighted, and Dromed spent the rest of the afternoon teaching us how to propel pits (as well as to relish the dates themselves).

Greyl couldn't spit. Lothar found a range of only a few steps. Borab couldn't spit at all because of his tusks. But I...well, I did all right, propelling date pits at least over half as far as Dromed—our undisputed champion. None of us ever came close to his range!

Thank heavens there were lots more date palms at the oasis. We spent many happy days munching heavenly dates and shooting pits. (Dromed always won: Camels are known to be unabashed spitters—pits or not!)

All this time, my Star patiently waited every night in the west, calling me to take up the Journey again, and I could sense a 'heaviness' (a certain urgency) to my Star Stone. I asked Dromed if he thought my Star would take us to the Land of Judea as his King's star did.

Dromed said maybe we had better go and see. I asked him if it wouldn't be hard for him to leave the oasis which had been his home for so long? He said that he felt it was time to go.

We asked Greyl to again scout a route to the west for us. She returned to report that two large river systems were to our west, and these areas would offer water and forage. The in-betweens would be hard for Lothar and me, but Borab and Dromed would probably do just fine.

I was a bit concerned about Dromed who was very old, but he assured me he could definitely make one more long desert crossing. (I believe he had hoped that his last trip would be to his King; but after all these years that was improbable, especially since Dromed's king lived in a totally different direction.)

Actually, this leg of our Journey was not that difficult, thanks to Greyl. We avoided human habitations near their populated river areas. Once again, we traveled only after dark.

Borab kept us supplied with the most unimaginable foods dug up from the earth. We learned to trust him (and not to look before eating them). We found that desert wanderers, like Borab, got much of their needed moisture from the fleshy tubers that were rooted out from under the sandy top soil. So gifted was he, he could smell and dig out buried water holes where we saw only dry, parched sand.

We finally left desert terrain and came into lands of greater diversity of form and vegetation. Greyl reported that we were nearing a great sea that bounded this area on the west. Dromed said it was the Mare Nostrum, and it bordered much of human civilization and cultures. (He had picked up this information from his King's conversations long ago.)

Greyl had found colonies of geese along the shores and water areas bordering the great sea, and they clued her into how really huge this sea was.

"If your Star leads you much farther west, Zar," she remarked, "you all will have to sprout either fins or wings!"

"Now that," commented Lothar, dryly, "should really be a challenge, a real adventure!"

As we got into a greener area, I asked Lothar if he ever longed for the mountains and meadows of the Northern Forests and the lush green of our youth.

He replied dreamily, "Oh, yes, there are many days I long for those homelands, but I knew long ago that a whole life of that sameness was not for me...I would not have missed all that I've seen and met on our Journey for anything. This adventure is worth it all—hardships, extremes of cold and hot, even those indescribable things that Borab has given us to eat."

I felt the same way, but with the addition of still hoping to meet a tall evergreen tree again!

CHAPTER 2

THE CEDAR MOUNTAINS

"Does anyone know if camels can swim?" I asked this of Dromed when we had arrived at the first of the two rivers that Greyl had surveyed.

Dromed couldn't answer that question because, in his experience, camels as a rule, encountered more deep sand than deep water—and had the feet to efficiently navigate only the former.

The answer was never demonstrated, because by the time we found the rivers, they were quite subdued in ferocity. Dromed waded in to prove a point (i.e., to prove that he could swim) but because of his long legs, he simply waded across. Lothar, Borab, and I did have to swim, because we were considerably shorter in legs. Borab, however, cheated. He grabbed Dromed's tail and was towed across.

By the time we had crossed the second river, we had entered that different land that I spoke of—more hills, more vegetation—and to Greyl's great relief, a reorientation of my Star! (We didn't have to sprout fins or wings!)

It happened at about the same time as my four-legged companions and I got the first sniff of real trees—Dromed's Cedar Mountains! Lothar and I almost cried for joy: we were so hungry for 'green' again.

That night, my Star shifted again to the south, and that shift coincided with our arrival at rather robust mountains, covered densely with the great cedars that Dromed had seen so long ago.

We traveled through and along these mountains wherever we could find a route, smelling both the wonderful incense of cedars and a bit of the tang of the sea to the west.

It was a kind of heaven to Lothar and me: recalling the northern pines of our early homelands. Even stumbling through the remains of some winter snows, we were ecstatic. He and I frolicked and slid around like youngsters, forgetting how glad we were (some seasons ago) when we safely left the high, snowy mountains that we hoped never to see again—mountain-goat (not 'ghost', I reminded myself!) territory.

No goats this time, but Greyl again spotted our trails southward through the cedars. Oh, Borab grumbled a bit: he missed his deserts. Dromed skidded around a bit, but assured us that we would parallel the Mare Nostrum and eventually come out into the Land of Judea. Was that where *my* Star led?

The big questions to me were—did my Star really duplicate the destination of Dromed's Kings? And was there a similar goal for this second Star? We had never sensed any ultimate goal for our journey, but there might be...and would it be revealed to us? We were, all five of us, so different in our perceptions that I wondered if we would individually—or collectively—know it when we saw it?

I posed these questions to my comrades and received five different perspectives, as I should have realized I would.

Lothar, the activist, thought the whole adventure was his goal.

Greyl, the altruist, believed that sharing her different perspectives and guidance to us was goal enough for her.

Borab, the opportunist, was 'along for the ride' (as well as new delicacies and new friends to appreciate them and him!)

Dromed, the idealist, had a goal. He hoped, this time, to see the miracle of the Prince of Peace.

As for me? The dreamer? Well, I just had to wait and see what or who was revealed. Or, on the other hand, I sought to be satisfied with the lifelong sufficiency of the Journey of the Star into the Great Unknown itself, and the miracle of meeting up with my very special companions, and the joy of that community. (After all, "Expectation is often better than Realization!")

But then, I was the dreamer and always had to wonder at the what if's or might be's? I had to chew and savor ideas the way Borab dealt with his delicacies. How very interesting. No, miraculous. That we five characters, with our different personalities and perspectives, had come together at just the right time to add ourselves to the mixture and take a Journey that I had originally believed to be uniquely mine.

"What does it matter?" laughed Lothar, "Just do it!"

"Look at the overview and map out the safest plan," added Greyl.

"Just enjoy everything—taste, smell, see, hear, and touch," commented Borab, snapping his tusks, "life is sensuous, delicious—eat it up!" (Click, click)

Dromed shook his head. "I'm not sure, but I *think* everything is goal-driven." (Dromed really did *think*!)

"How very un-camel," I replied. "What if?"

The others all stopped and laughed, and Lothar gently nipped me.

"Ease up, Zar," he said. "Sometimes your thinking is larger (and heavier) than you are. How often have you reminded us that the Journey *is* the goal! Now, let's *do* the Journey."

We moved on. Amazingly, Dromed began to recognize our route as his route (and that of his Kings) of long ago. He was now on familiar ground. Apparently, things changed slowly in this land, and he remembered many details that he thought never to see again.

In the mountains, we traveled by day to see our way, but when we arrived at more inhabited lower lands, we had to travel by night again, holing up by day to avoid human observation.

Dromed remembered that his caravan, long ago, had done the same, for the same reasons, using darkness as protection.

My Star grew ever closer, and seemed to be almost overhead. I realized that we were nearing the completion of our Journey, and although tremendously excited by the prospect, I was growing concerned. No…afraid of a letdown and an unknown aftermath.

Lothar kept nudging me to "quit thinking and just live in the present." But, I believe, all five of us were both excited and concerned. After all, we really were no longer young; Lothar and I had grown old together, and the rest were quite mature and seasoned when we met up. The Journey had been long and, at times, quite strenuous. Probably, none of us would ever be able to return 'home', if we even knew where 'home' was and how to get there.

Now, in mid-winter, this night was moonless and frosty. The land lay still and sleeping. My Star, directly overhead, seemed to send down long rays of sparkle much like a frosty, luminous mist.

Then it happened. I was suddenly aware of the tinkling of 'star chimes.' I had heard them so long ago, before my Star had shifted once in the heavens.

"Do you hear the Star?" I whispered, awestruck, fearing even to break the surrounding silence.

Lothar, Borab, and Dromed almost froze in their tracks. They each cocked their heads. Obviously, they heard something.

"Is that your Star Music?" whispered Lothar back to me.

I saw the bristles rise up on Borab's spine.

Dromed was head up, drinking in some sound or scent.

We all stood speechless. Then, a flurry of wings—and Greyl dropped down among us.

"The night is full of music," she said, "the earth seems to be holding its breath." And, looking around at us, she added, "I seem to be the only living thing moving at this moment."

It was a moment that went on forever, it seemed. None of us moved. Lothar and I sat where we were, heads up and searching, like Dromed.

The only sound then that came from the earth was a lamb bleating in the distance…a wee, newborn lamb? In *mid-winter*?

CHAPTER 3

THE MISTS OF TIME

The darkness and the stars faded into the new day. The chimes of starlight faded into the mists of dawn. We found ourselves in a vast field of frost—a clump of puzzled animals searching for a safe passage for our journey.

Dromed was the first to speak. "This way," he said, softly, confidently.

We followed him, never questioning nor doubting his assurance. The frost became deep mist, which hid us from any other creatures of the morning. Greyl rode on Borab's back, his broad, rough surface the only one that could support her in comfort.

Dromed stopped suddenly, and the rest of us, following him closely in the mist, piled up on him before we knew it. Lothar barged into me and Borab into Lothar. He gave a muffled "yip," as tusk met tail.

"Oops, sorry!" Said Borab, spitting out a tuft of fur.

Greyl was launched into the mist and landed on Dromed, who looked around in amazement at the tangle of his compatriots.

He had stopped before a wall of stones that blocked our path. "Can you three manage to get over this wall without falling all over each other?" he said in amusement. He stepped over the wall with no problem, Greyl still on top.

Lothar leaped easily. But I had to boost Borab, whose bulk and short legs limited his upward mobility.

"This wall is human territory, Dromed! Are you sure you are going the right way?" I asked, puzzled by his confidence at this moment.

"Trust me," he answered, "something is guiding me at this moment although this is new territory for me. I trust my intuition. Please believe me. We are on the right course...but to whom or what, I don't know."

We followed obediently, if not warily (for sudden stops). All through our Journey one or another of our partners had stepped up to the leadership of the group when needed, usually without asking, and we had always trusted each other's ability or talent (even Borab's!)

Now, Dromed seemed completely in charge, and I was grateful, being at a loss when my Star 'stood still', so to speak. No one or anything had clued me in to the immediate goal, if any. And, I had learned, if Dromed saw or felt something, to pay attention. Now, I was exceedingly relieved...and curious.

It wasn't particularly easy following a white camel in a white-out, but, at least, my big black bulk would be easy for Lothar and Borab to follow.

So when Dromed stopped suddenly—again—our collisions were not quite as dramatic as last time—comic but not catastrophic.

"Oh, no, not again," sighed Dromed. But he held his ground until we collected ourselves. Our Journey of muddling around in a fog was stopped, and the stop was at a looming structure, ahead.

It appeared to be a type of shed, a lean-to of old wood timbers that formed the open door of an earth-block structure (like many of the human structures in this part of the world). It was a rough shelter—perhaps a stable.

Dromed moved forward, then quietly stood in front of it...peering into the opening and then turning his head to look at us. We had moved up beside him to also look in. Although none of us had the faintest idea what he saw, or what we were to look for. We all seemed at a loss for what to do next.

Then, a voice from within said, tentatively, "Hello? Who's there? Please...who is there?"

None of us spoke up, because we didn't seem to know which of us was in charge. Apparently, Dromed had decided at that moment to abdicate his leadership in the face of a forthright challenge.

I spoke, (feeling that maybe it was my role again to represent us, as no one else uttered a peep): "Hello...I am Prince Althazar—and these are my partners: Prince Lothar, Greyl, Borab, and Dromed, a Royal Camel. We are on a Journey of the Star to the Great Unknown and that Journey seems to have ended right here!"

It sounded a bit thin, but, in my estimation, it told it all. Besides, what else could I say in the face of no face, just a voice. "We come in Peace," I added.

"Did you say Dromed, a Royal Camel?" came the voice. And then emerged a shape from the shelter. The shape of a donkey. Very old and gray, yet the voice was strong: "Dromed? Did you say, Dromed?"

"Solomon?" exclaimed Dromed, rearing up his head and cracking it on the door frame…"Oh, my God…this again?" Then he began to laugh, and to cry, both at once. He put his nose down to gently touch that of the donkey.

"Dromed?"

"Solomon?"

"Oh, can it be? Is this the goal? The end?"

Dromed was in shock; so were we. We silently stood in amazement. We had all heard Dromed's story and this meeting of the donkey and the camel again seemed miraculous and awesome!

"Come in, please…oh, do come in," said the donkey, "And, Dromed…mind your head: Let's not go through all *that* again!"

We squeezed through the doorway to find a roomy place within. Visibility was not too good, but the misty fog seemed to shed some brightness to the interior. The donkey moved back to survey our motley crew in front of him—Bear, Wolf, Wild Boar, Goose, and Camel (whose head was mindfully lowered).

"I'm afraid that I'm almost blind with age," said Solomon, "but the lower the light, the more I can see, so this shed suits me well. It is probably hard on you all. Please sit. I'm sorry I have no food to offer."

We all mumbled that it was just fine; we could see quite well, and thanked him for his courtesy. We sat down comfortably on the straw-strewn floor, and waited for this next chapter of amazing coincidences or miracles to unfold.

CHAPTER 4

SOLOMON

I noticed that the donkey, Solomon, was trembling, and I wondered if our presence here was a bit too much for him.

Dromed was busy folding down into his 'sit' position, which was always amusing to the rest of us, as it was an improbable restructuring of angles, but as he was almost too tall for the shed, folding up (or down) was definitely in order.

This put all of us in what I called, the Peaceful Intent position, and surely showed nothing of threat to the donkey.

"Solomon," I asked, "you seem to be uncomfortable; I can assure you that we mean no harm. Would you be more at ease sitting down, also?"

Solomon lowered his head slightly, and replied, "Oh, I am fine, really. At my age getting down and getting up are major efforts and I stand as the lesser of two discomforts. The shaking? Like my eyesight and my teeth, my strength is disappearing also. Furthermore, I have never been in close proximity to a Bear, or a Wolf, or a Wild Boar! Donkeys are usually on the low end of the animal food chain for those animals."

We all nodded agreeably, and our wolf Lothar said, "As my partners know, I long ago announced that I should never eat anyone who could carry on intelligent conversation with me. Please be at ease. I come as a friend."

I added, "I'm pretty much a vegetarian, with the exception of fish."

Borab added, "I'm a gourmet of sorts and…"

Solomon interjected abruptly, "And that leaves me out. I'm too old and stringy!"

We all laughed comfortably, and as Greyl was often to say, a sense of humor and laughter again saved the day.

I told Solomon the story of the Journey of the Star, recounting some of the more vital *befores*, *durings*, and now, *afters*. I added that my Star had stopped here, and all of us were wondering if this was the end—which none of us ever really much imagined or comprehended—or thought we would find.

Solomon listened attentively and with my last statement said, "And you are surely wondering, but are probably too polite to ask: Why does this incredible Journey of a lifetime, this dream, end with a donkey? Why a lowly little donkey? Do I hold some key to your mystery? Am I really the end, or only the beginning, of your dream?"

Dromed said softly, "Something has led me twice to this country, in two different locations, and to you. And something led my partners to me, thence to you. Perhaps if you tell us your complete story, it well may be that you are the beginning and the end."

I added seriously, "Dromed has said it so well. Lothar, Greyl, Borab, and I have traveled long and far to reach this place and we firmly believe that you are the key."

And so, Solomon began his story (referring to himself, as Solomon):

Life began for Solomon the day he fell in love. Oh, it really began before that in a donkey way—with growing up from being a foal to full young strength, halter, and riding-pad trained. But Solomon had long since forgotten most of those early days. They were but a distant memory. He only really began to count his life from the day he first saw his Lady—and realized that she was the love of his life!

He saw her coming down the path to the donkey paddock. She was with two men—one the donkey-master, the other a tall, older man who held the arm of the Lady in a way of gentleness and of a love that there could be no mistaking. He must be her husband, thought Solomon.

Solomon took this all in, even though his attention was fully on the Lady. In his eyes, she seemed to almost float down the path in radiant beauty.

Solomon was resting his head on the gate; the other donkeys were milling around in the background probably acting like young fools, while he, Solomon, was waiting in all his grace and maturity for what he knew would be a new destiny.

The Lady moved towards him with her hand extended and, when she arrived at the gate, Solomon gently placed his nose in her hand and looked deeply into his love's eyes. Her eyes were so deep and beautiful, he felt weak.

"Oh, what a beauty," she said in a voice like the bells of heaven, thought Solomon. (While he and the other animals easily understood most of a human's language, the ability was never two-ways. Humans never really understand the language of other species, even now.)

"He is the most refined and graceful donkey I've ever seen!" she continued.

The older man beamed adoringly at the Lady. The donkey-master remarked that Solomon was smaller than most of the other donkeys, but he was very well proportioned and would be very capable and strong.

The Lady wasn't finished, "Look at his neat feet and hooves—he is most certainly a special creature!"

Solomon made a note to check out his feet as soon as possible. He had spent a lot of time checking out his reflection in the water-trough: glowing silver coat, black mane, but he had never given much thought to his feet and hooves. He did notice that the Lady had neat hooves, err, feet, herself. But then, everything about her was neat and graceful—tall for a female, very young, elegant, willowy—obviously much younger than her husband, and also, obviously, the apple of his eye.

And speaking of apples, there, in her other hand, appeared an apple which she gave to Solomon. "Love is an apple," thought Solomon; "our love is sealed with an apple. My Lady, I am yours forever."

He felt faint, but it would never do (in a business deal) for the merchandise to fall down dead before the deal was done! Or even after!

The husband smiled happily and handed over the coins of purchase to the donkey-master, who opened the gate, tied a rope to Solomon's halter and handed the rope to the husband.

"Oh," said the Lady, "please let me ride him home!"

The man lifted her up upon Solomon and gathered up the rope to lead them away.

To Solomon, the Lady's weight felt light as an angel, and he put forth a special effort to move with grace and smoothness worthy of an angel.

"Why, he is the smoothest, gentlest ride I've ever had," she said, her voice like music to Solomon, who vowed to carry her always in grace and safety. "What shall we call him, my dearest?"

<ins>That</ins> would do very well, thought Solomon, but he knew he was carrying his passion a bit far. "Solomon," he said, out loud, knowing full well that humans could not possibly understand—or even hear him. "My name is SOLOMON!"

"Husband," said his Lady, "We shall call him 'Solomon', he looks so very wise…so soulful…Solomon is his new name! I just know it!"

Solomon almost fainted again, but love revitalized him, and he knew that there would be some form of communication possible between his Lady and himself. (And so there was, always, although not in an exchange of words out loud).

The home that the three of them went to was in a small village. The house fronted on a street and had a large walled yard—almost a field in back. The house was low and long with one end that served as the husband's work area; the other end, as the living area.

The work area for the man was partly opened into the back yard and shaded by deep roofs. The man worked in wood, and his tools and materials were neatly stacked under the roofs.

There was a shed attached to the family end of the house that faced into the backyard also. This shed was where Solomon was led. It was to be his home. Apparently, the two humans had gone to some effort to make it cool and comfortable and cozy.

There was a half-door that led in to the yard, and Solomon discovered as soon as the humans left him, there was another half-door that opened into the house and the food and eating area for the family. (The shed had not been designed originally for livestock.)

That house door was covered on the top half by a blanket or some heavy cloth which Solomon put his nose around and discovered a peg of wood that, when lifted out of a round slot, allowed the top half of the door to swing open, into the house. Oops!

It was a bit of a shock to his Lady when, after stowing her donkey, she returned to her kitchen to find his head in her house!

She gave a gasp of amazement and amusement that brought her husband very quickly to her side. They both laughed until they had to sit down. The husband said, between laughs, "Well, I guess we have a family room. Complete with our first 'new son'! Whoever said that donkeys were dumb? I'll bet he can open the outside door of his shed, too."

Solomon knew that he could and would as soon as he'd checked that out! No, donkeys were not slow and stupid. He believed that, through history, it probably had been to their advantage to appear that way.

His Lady added, "I wonder how our first-born will like sharing his family (and his house) with a donkey. I do so hope he shall find Solomon as beautiful and delightful as I do! He will ride him when he's old enough!"

That was the first indication to Solomon that his family was going to 'foal' in the future. The garments of the time were fulsome and they hid a lot. And his Lady was tall, graceful, and carried herself quite well. Solomon would have never guessed her 'condition', but then, he was still very young and unworldly and was only knowledgeable about donkeys.

So life—and days—passed. The husband was busy with his business of working and selling wood pieces to his friends and customers. Solomon's Lady was busy in her work area, cooking and sewing and visiting with her friends and relatives. (Everyone seemed to be related to everyone else, somehow, in this human society.) And Solomon found time to keep company with both, inside and outside, as well as carry his Lady around whenever she went out.

Visitors to the wood shop considered him quite a character, and he was even more of a sensation in the kitchen. Solomon's Lady was so good-humored and happy and amused that all who stopped into the house joined in with her amusement at Solomon's presence—at least his head's presence. A lot of apples and fruit came his way. It was agreed that he had a very wise look and seemed to listen to their conversations, ready to join in.

(Of course, said Solomon—although they couldn't understand him—I am joining in, and I do have some very ripe opinions...if you only knew!)

The days went by happily. Solomon's Lady and her husband discussed the 'coming event' often, and both were very excited and happy, but as expected, a bit nervous, too. (There were also, many other references to religious ideas that Solomon really didn't understand.)

Solomon's Lady got bigger and bigger, although she still carried it well. She was so merry and playful still, and sang and danced around the kitchen when her husband was in his shop.

"Solomon, my pet," she said to him, "you won't tell anyone about the singing or dancing will you? They might consider me improper or not serious enough!" Solomon nodded and shook his head, which he believed, would cover all questions. He loved to hear her sing and wished he could dance, too. He was so happy!

Her husband would not let Solomon's Lady go out alone on the donkey when she got really large. When she went shopping she rode on Solomon, but her husband demanded she go with a friend, or wait for him. Lady protested; she was young and healthy and felt fine...and she loved riding out on Solomon!

"No, my love," said her husband as sternly as he could, trying to hide the adoration in his eyes, "later, when you are a bit less top-heavy on Solomon. We do not want any falls or mishaps!"

Solomon knew how graceful and competent his Lady really was, and he also knew that he would never, never allow any accident to happen to her! But he also respected the love and the fears for her safety that the husband had for his Lady. He also noted the so-called 'social constraints' of his community that dealt with females. They pretty well did what their males told them to do. It was a 'social' position that seemed to Solomon to often reduce females to a different level, or unimportance, much like animals in this part of the world.

Did males ever really listen to either? Well he did! Solomon, a lowly donkey, listened and respected all creatures! Probably an unpopular notion or a totally inconceivable idea at any time, although, maybe a day might come when such a dream would be realized.

Chapter 5

Silent Night, Holy Night

There came a day when the delightful life that Solomon so treasured was turned upside down. This happened when his Lady was almost at her time.

The husband was ordered by civil authorities to travel to another town, far to the south, to register for a 'human-count'. Solomon overheard a lot of discussion about this, but it was far from his comprehension. (Why would anyone want to count humans?)

There were, of course, hurried plans made for this journey. Someone or some of the many friends or relatives had to be asked to take care of the house and the workshop. Only the sparest of clothing and supplies could be carried, as Solomon would have to carry everything, as well as his very ready-to-give-birth Lady.

The burden didn't bother him; he knew that he was up to the task. His greatest anxiety was for the comfort of his Lady, in such an awkward, uncomfortable condition. The husband would have to walk and carry any extra belongings.

The three of them started off as soon as they could, but making much distance was going to be hard, because his Lady was obviously very uncomfortable, even though Solomon tried his best to smooth out the ordeal. She didn't cry or make any noise or complaint, but Solomon could feel her shifting her weight to relieve her distress. He hurt for her, and he knew her husband did also.

His only comfort to her was to sing or hum to her—and he hoped she could hear him. She must have heard or felt something, because her hands kept stroking his neck and her fingers would tie and untie his mane, probably in an attempt to distract herself.

The husband had tried to purchase another donkey for himself, but none was available for the little money he could spare. They had very little to purchase a night's lodging, and the traveling went so slowly that there were all too many stops for rest and lodging.

Solomon lost track of the days they were on the road. He only knew that very, very soon, there would be four of them, and he dreaded the thought of his beautiful and regal Lady birthing on the side of some dusty road like a common beast. From the worry-stricken face of the husband, and his constant hand on the back of his Lady, Solomon knew that they all knew how desperate the time was!

They could not just camp out. It was winter and the nights were frosty; they had to find lodging in the next small town which was, thankfully, their destination for the 'human-count'. Solomon was sure they simply could not have gone another day!

Darkness was falling fast; and with it, frost…for the wind had dropped, and the cold settled down in a brightness that seemed to reproduce the stars. Stars were a blanket above, frost a blanket below.

Overhead hung an even brighter glow, from an even brighter cluster of stars that seemed to pave their way through the dark streets of the little town. The starlight made the dusty town look almost beautiful.

Solomon's Lady was shivering, even though the husband had long since wrapped her in his robe.

They stopped before the door of the only inn that they found on the far edge of the town. The husband knocked on the door. It seemed a very long time before anyone appeared to answer his knock.

Light streamed from behind a man (probably the innkeeper) when the door opened a crack. Every window in every building including the inn, had shutters drawn to keep out the cold, so the sudden light was startling and all three of them jumped.

Before the husband even said a word, the innkeeper said he was sorry but every room was filled…there was no room left in his inn!

The husband said, as the door started to close, "Please sir, my wife is so tired and sick from our long journey. I fear her time has come and…"

He never finished the sentence. The door closed, and the three of them were left stranded on the street.

But then, a light appeared in the doorway again, and a voice said softly, "Did I hear you say your wife's time had come?"

"Yes, oh, yes," answered the husband, desperation in his voice, "Is there, possibly, any shed or just any cover that we can find for the night?"

A woman stepped forth, carrying a lantern. "Come with me," she said.

The husband led Solomon, following behind the glowing lantern. His Lady gave a long sigh—the only sound that she made during the last part of their journey. She is so regal, thought Solomon; so strong and brave!

The woman with the lantern led them around the back of the inn to a hillside, black against the luminous sky. There she entered a cave. Her light illuminated a stable, fragrant of hay, and looming in the shadows, other beasts.

There was a ewe and two lambs, two milk cows, an old, old donkey and some chickens. They rustled and murmured upon being awakened, and their eyes glowed in the light of the lantern.

The cave was warm, almost comfortable, from the heat of the beasts that called it home. Solomon thought it a splendid and very hospitable place to spend the night. (Better than a closed-down, stuffy, human-place!)

The woman carefully set down the lantern and went to help the husband lift Solomon's Lady off his back. They helped her to a stack of straw, and as she sank down gratefully, another deep sigh escaped.

The woman clucked sympathetically upon seeing just how large Lady was, and went about collecting more straw to make a pallet.

The husband removed Solomon's blanket and laid it on the straw under his cloak, which he folded over on top of Lady as she lay down (not an easy job in her condition).

The woman went to get fresh water and returned with a clean bucket-full and some bread from the house, as well as clean cloths. The husband was stroking and wiping Lady's face and Solomon nuzzled her damp hair while trying to croon soft, comforting songs to her. She smiled at him and at her husband.

The woman asked the husband if he wanted her to stay and help. From the house, a man's voice sounded, shouting to the woman to come in. The husband thanked her for her thoughtfulness but declined her assistance. Solomon had the feeling that the woman was vastly relieved, although she volunteered to bring some more food and things in the morning.

The lantern that she left made the stable very comforting, but there also was a bright glow from the mouth of the cave that lighted up everything, as well as warming up the whole place. Undeniably, a great radiance filled the stable, coupled with great anticipation and peace. "What a night," thought Solomon, "what a place!"

There, that night in that place, Solomon's Lady went into deep labor—and she, with the help of her husband, delivered her child. Sometime after midnight, a son was born. A cry of new life echoed in the cave, and it seemed that all the beasts and Solomon cried out also—and laughed and wept all at once.

Certainly, Lady and the husband did!

But this night of nights was not finished. From the distance came the sound of singing...and bells...and music...and the sound of many voices, growing ever closer. The husband and Solomon felt a prickle of anxiety.

At the cave's opening, the voices hushed in near-reverence. Tentatively, almost fearfully, a group of local shepherds and their lads shuffled in, eyes big in wonder.

The aroma of damp, raw wool and dusty feet, sweaty hands and cold night air entered into the stable to mix with hay and beast. Solomon, ever after, would recall that incredible scene at the mere whiff of these odors.

Was this a miraculous night, or what?

There was something Holy afoot, explained the shepherds to the husband—and they quietly, and in great excitement and joy, told their story. Something about Herald Angels and a special Holy Birth...and words that Solomon, for all his trying, couldn't quite understand. "Wasn't the birth of any new life Holy?" He wondered. Then he thought about his beautiful, regal Lady, and her gentle and strong adoring husband, and all the events that led up to this night, this place, this birth.

"It must be special," thought Solomon. "It must be extra-special Holy!" And he, Solomon, was part of it all! He wondered if a little donkey could ever be a smidgen Holy? Probably not, he concluded, standing there beside his Lady, crooning soft songs of love and comfort. After all, <u>this</u> was about as Holy as it gets—or ever needs to be!

The human talk of Kings and Princes, Messiahs and Prophets, even Angels, swirled around Solomon like so much chaff. Stable talk was always much more down to earth: wonder, contentment, glowing eyes and stars, warm fragrant hay and a beautiful, though exhausted Lady cradling a wee-born in her arms. This was the real stuff earth was made of. Heaven could come later—as for a Prince of Peace? Again, Solomon concluded that this precious, hushed, joyful stable scene was as peace-filled as it gets!

He bent down to nuzzle the newborn Prince of Peace—and smelled and tasted the greatest of all gifts: Life...and the love that gives and nourishes it!

CHAPTER 6

AFTER THE STAR STOOD STILL

A long, hushed silence fell over our company as we listened to Solomon's story. He stood not speaking, his filmy eyes wet and staring at some unseen memory from a time long past. Dromed, Lothar, Greyl, Borab, and I waited respectfully for his story to continue as, indeed, it would have to. We had been taken with him right up to the special moment and dropped there, unexpectedly.

Maybe time had stood still that night; maybe, right now, it did the same.

I finally spoke to Solomon in gentle tones, in case he was far away from the present: "Solomon, my friend, go on, please. We really are hanging on your every word!"

Solomon seemed to awaken from his reveries, and said in what sounded like a complete change of tone, "It is nearing day's end, is it not? We have used a whole day, and it is now evening. I must go up to the gate and meet my Lady."

"What do you mean?" I said, "Is your Lady still here...or what?"

Solomon brought his focus back to us and explained, "Oh, I am still here with my Lady, although because of my age I cannot carry her anymore. She has moved me down to this pleasant spring area at the lower end of her property. Her husband had bought this addition to their land before he died.

"She brings me warm mash every evening. You see, my teeth are long gone, and I can no longer chew hay and grain. My Lady comes to visit and feed me every evening, or if she cannot come down, a lovely young girl, a relative of hers, brings me the mash. Once a week, the girl comes into the shed to change the straw. Retirement for me has been very sweet, except I miss carrying my Lady and being her special donkey!"

I replied, "It certainly sounds as though you are still her special donkey!"

"Not like the old days," mused Solomon, "not like the old days." He stiffly hobbled out of the stable and disappeared.

We were rather in a daze ourselves. Lothar said, "What do you make of this? The husband is dead, and where is the son? Greyl, can you go out and scout around outside and find Solomon? Tell us where we are; get the lay of the land!"

"Good idea," I added. The presence of any one of us might be a bit of a shock if we were observed outside.

I realized that we had never seen where we were or what area we were in, relative to human habitation. I was always wary of human contact, as were Lothar and Borab. Dromed, of course, being a 'domesticated animal' had no such wariness. Still, we were an unusual company of animals, and not being native to this land, extremely obvious. (Dromed the exception).

We had arrived in a mist, spent a whole day inside, and now it was coming on night. We didn't know where we were. Thank goodness for Greyl. She would once more be our eyes and ears.

Greyl left to scout our whereabouts. It was not dark yet, but the night would be coming on soon.

Light filtering through holes in the walls gave us enough visibility to see one another. I noticed that my partners were restless and wary. Perhaps when Greyl returned and gave us more information about our area, we could feel more comfortable. (Wild animals are always conscious of being in potential traps.)

However, with Borab and Lothar, the restlessness turned out to be plain old hunger.

Borab asked, "Do you think I could sneak out after it is thoroughly dark and forage for some tasty morsels? Surely, with all these farms and fields around, there must be some food left behind after the harvest."

Lothar replied, "I believe I'll try around the houses."

Dromed interrupted him, "Where there are humans, there is always leftover food…it's called *garbage*. But look out, little brother—the stray dogs usually get there first…and they are unruly outlaws!"

Lothar curled his lip and bristled his ruff, "I'll give them a taste of unruly wolf!"

"Oh, for goodness sakes," I admonished, "Don't start anything. If I have to rescue any one or all of you, there will be a riot! I doubt if a Great Bear has appeared in ages. Remember that we are here with Peaceful Intent! Do wait until after midnight and after Greyl and Solomon have returned, please!"

Dromed and I were not particularly interested in food. We had so much to think about—me, the Dreamer; Dromed, the Idealist. We two, always chasing Ideas and *what ifs*: waiting and thinking, thinking and waiting.

Lothar and Borab agreed to hold off, and both lay down to nap away the time. (Any growling that I heard was from the stomachs of my two hungry partners.)

At dusk, Greyl came fluttering in, bringing the scent of cold fresh air into our stuffy little shed. I suddenly had a pang of hunger. Hunger for the great evergreens of the mountain forests, for lush green meadows, and rushing streams. I wondered why the Star had taken my companions and me so far away, into strange, arid lands, into the very heartland of human society. I wondered why it was here that the Star stood still—and we, also.

"That," said Greyl shaking her feathers into alignment, "is one lucky donkey! He has a cozy grove of trees around a marsh, not a common thing in this country. A private stable and dinner served every evening by a very lovely, attentive lady who visits with him while he dines! We should all be so favored in *our* retirement!"

The four of us exchanged glances. Apparently, Solomon had the best of all possible worlds, and maybe, domestication wasn't as horrible as we had thought. Greyl reported that the lands around here were inhabited mainly in clusters of towns. Much of the area was open land or farmed fields.

Solomon's description of his Lady's house was accurate. This place that he—we—were in was just down a hill from the back courtyard.

Greyl said that foraging for our various foods would be safe in the darkness. Few humans were about after dark. Responsible, honest humans carried lanterns. Those that didn't, well, they deserved whatever they bumped into in their foraging.

Lothar, Borab, and I laughed, imagining how it would be for a thieving human to run into any one (or all of us) in the dark of night!

Solomon came in at that point, looking a lot less shaky, and with a dreamy, but contented, look on his face. He nodded and said, "Forgive me for being rude, but I am very tired and would like to sleep tonight. I will continue the story in the morning." And he carefully lay down in a corner and was asleep before we could say a word.

"Let's see if we can find something to eat," said Lothar and Borab, almost in chorus. They collided at the doorway and got stuck momentarily in their mad rush to get out.

Greyl and I laughed, and Dromed said, "If I had done such a hasty exit with those two, we should have never gotten untangled!" He unfolded himself and went out to browse.

I followed after raising an eyebrow at Greyl. It was too dark now for her to see me, but intuitive that she was, said, "I'll go out before dawn and find some food. Zar, keep a listen for our two hungry warriors. I fear for Lothar, mainly…he isn't nearly as spry as he thinks he is. Age is showing a bit in his joints, though not in his heart!"

I had to admit that all that was true of every one of us. Long seasons on the Journey had slowed us down physically, but the fire in our hearts burned hotly.

I ambled out into a crisp winter night. My Star blazed directly overheard. I touched my Star Stone and I said out loud, "Yes, I guess we have arrived. You have led us safely to this place; for whom or what I do not know. But the Journey is an awesome sufficiency…and I am thankful."

CHAPTER 7

THE BOYS' NIGHT OUT ON THE TOWN

'Lunch' was on my mind. I decided to follow Borab's scent-trail, knowing how efficiently he found food—and, usually, the kind of food I preferred. Unlike most animals, Borab loved to share his bounty.

I caught up with him a fair distance from Solomon's stable. He, of course, knew of my coming long before we actually saw one another. He clicked his tusks in greeting and dug out a root or 'something' and shoved it towards me. "Bet you'll like this," he said, rooting a furrow, turning out more of the 'somethings'.

Whatever it was, it was tangy and good. Borab showed me where to look and dig. "What do you call this?" I asked.

"Food," was the reply. "I don't name them, I just eat them!"

I laughed; Borab was a droll delight. I hoped these were leftovers from a harvest, and we weren't decimating some poor farmer's winter crop. I was sure that Borab had no such mental restraints.

From the town on the hill suddenly came sounds of yelps, barks, howls, and cries.

"Oh, no!" I exclaimed, "It's Lothar. He is tangling with the town dogs. I told him to watch out!"

I took off in a fast gallop towards the racket. I didn't wait for Borab. Lothar was my oldest and dearest friend, and I would always rush to his aid, as he would for me.

Bears can really cover ground quickly, even old ones like me. I ran straight towards the sound, which seemed to be increasing in volume. As I ran, I growled, and by the time I came up to the battle, I was in a full Bear Bellow!

The sound of my roar preceded me down the town's street. Lantern-lights appeared in houses, but no one ventured outside that I could see. Who would dare?

My fiercest Bear Bellow scattered the forces before me, and the cries and yelps dispersed in all directions. I barreled to a halt before one lone warrior: Lothar.

"Why did you break it up?" he exclaimed, "I was just warming to my finest effort. But, wow! What a magnificent sound you can make when you put on your Bear Act!"

A hissing, growling, snorting Borab galloped in. "Am I too late?" he gasped, "Have I missed all the carnage?"

"Oh, you are both too much," I roared. "Let's get out of here before someone gets hurt."

We trotted swiftly out of town, leaving behind a legend to be magnified by a host of different spectators. In my own agitation, I gave one parting shot of defiance—one more night-splitting roar. My finest Bear Bellow. I, too, had just warmed up!

We took an indirect way back to Solomon's stable, just in case we were followed. Everything seemed very silent now in the town, and no scent of anyone following us could be picked up by super-nose: Borab. (Lothar and I were very keen in the nose department, but Borab could pick up on things even we missed.)

A much-fluffed up Greyl met us at the stable door. When in extreme agitation her feathers seemed to stand on end, making her look larger than life.

"Well," she said dryly, "You boys certainly had a night on the town. From the sound of it, Peaceful Intent was somehow lost in a wash of 'discontent'! Did any of you happen to stumble across a big gentle, harmless camel in your frantic evening's debauch?"

"Dromed?" I asked, "You mean Dromed is lost?"

"Well, he hasn't come home yet," she replied.

We decided to go out and search for him, but, first, I directed Lothar to stay back with Greyl and Solomon. Even in the dark of the night, I could see that Lothar had been roughed up, and I could smell blood. He agreed without protest—a sure sign that he was a little worse for wear.

Borab and I immediately picked up Dromed's scent-trail and followed it as fast as we could. The trail took us once more closer to human habitation than I would want. Field forage was one thing, human farm forage was another. Were we all becoming a rogue pack of thieves in our old age? Somehow, I didn't think my Star would ever lead me into pilfering like the stray dogs for whom Lothar had such contempt. But I did humbly admit that ethics and ideas were hard to retain on an empty stomach!

We found Dromed snorting and gurgling in a hurt-camel way. He was stomping and straining, caught in something at the edge of a storage shed.

I called to him softly so that he would not make any noise of surprise by our arrival.

"Oh, thank God," he sobbed, "I am so glad you are here. I have my foot caught in some kind of snare…and the harder I pull, the tighter it gets!"

My memory went back to the time Lothar and I had rescued Greyl. She, also, had been caught in a snare, a loop of strong line that pulled on a slipknot (Greyl had described) when a victim stumbled through it. I told Dromed to stop struggling and explained that Borab and I would open the loop and free his foot. That was easier said than done.

All Dromed's struggles had pulled the snare so tightly that it was cutting into his ankle, and for the second time this night, I smelled blood. I could not get a claw under the loop, nor could Borab with his tusk, although he managed to snap off one of them in the effort. For the third time this night, I smelled blood. Without intending, all we did was to hurt Dromed more, although he tried not to show it.

I tried gnawing through the tethered end, but it was a hard, nasty-tasting 'something' that rasped against my teeth. Borab had the same result. Our teeth were no match for this material.

I tried pulling on the tethered end, but even my huge weight didn't budge it. The tough, sinewy snare seemed to be attached to a round 'something' imbedded in the wall of the shed.

Dromed was standing in patient despair and pain; Borab was ripping at the wall with his remaining tusks. I pushed him away before he tore off another of his precious tusks, and I went after the wooden wall, full force, with my claws, prodigious weapons that I had never used before in any anger or hostility.

I literally tore that wall to shreds and the tether with it. Dromed was free, although still wearing the snare and its loose end as a trailing-line.

Twice in one night I had used my bear equipment to aid a friend, and I wondered what else I could employ as my birthright. I guess I had never given much thought to my strength or endowments. (It all felt rather good!)

We carefully escorted Dromed back to Solomon's stable, trying to keep him from stumbling over the hobbling-line. He was very shaky and limping badly, but with our encouragement and gentle assistance, we made it back.

We were a sorry-looking lot that limped in at dawn: Dromed with a swollen, bloody forefoot; Borab with part of a tusk missing; I with several broken claws, joining a rumpled Lothar with patches of fur missing and dried blood in various places. Indeed, it was some night on the town!

Greyl surveyed us in speechless awe. She didn't even give us a tongue-lashing. She actually clucked rather gently at each of us in turn and said how glad she was to see us safely back. Through all this, Solomon slept soundly, wheezing in slow breaths and twitching in dreams (probably of his younger donkey days when he was confident and strong—as we all dreamed, nowadays).

After a bit of a rest, we went after Dromed's snare, each in turn, trying to get it off his foot. Each, in turn, failed to bite or claw through that thing. (Lothar lost two front teeth in his turn. Good Lord, more blood!) Throughout this ordeal, Dromed patiently endured it without a sound. He really was a King's Camel, and bore himself with nobility and dignity.

Finally, in desperation, Borab exclaimed: "Mud! Let's get Dromed out to that wet area beyond this stable. Cold mud will soothe his foot and maybe reduce the swelling and pain!"

Good idea, we all concurred; bad idea sighed Dromed—he didn't think he could get up and walk outside.

With me on one side and stout, solid Borab on the other, we shoved and pushed Dromed out of the stable, got him up on three legs and eased him down to the frost-encrusted marsh. There, with one of us on either side of him, we cautiously let down his swollen foot into the cold mud.

Almost immediately, Dromed gave a sigh of relief and stopped shaking.

Lothar, who had followed us, thought that water and mud might be the answer to his own discomfort. He found a sufficiently deep place to roll into and soothe his own wounds.

Borab, although only hurting from an abbreviated tusk, decided to join in the mud party—as it was his idea. I lay down to soak my throbbing forepaws. All in all, we were a strange sight, I presumed, and maybe an altogether fitting aftermath of "her boys' night out on the town," as Greyl called it thereafter!

Before too long, Greyl and Solomon emerged from the stable. Both seemed to be highly amused at our mud party. Apparently, Greyl had reported on all the incredible adventures of the night—at least all that she knew.

She took off to scout the town and activities, leaving Solomon to us, or visa versa. He checked out the trailing-end of the snare around Dromed's foot, and said it was no wonder none of us could pry it off! He declared: "Teeth, claws, and tusks would be useless in trying to break such a tough, hardened sinew." (Obviously!)

Chapter 8

Taking a Chance On Trust

Solomon's solution to the problem of freeing Dromed from the pain and danger of a snare digging into his ankle was both simple and complex: he had to take his friend up to the evening feeding, and hope that Solomon's Lady would notice his discomfort, and in her human way—undo what another human had contrived.

"Too dangerous," said we wild creatures. "Good idea," said our domestic camel. "Do any of you have a better idea? Heavens knows, you have all done your best. You've sacrificed tusk, tooth, and claw to free me. Solomon's Lady is my best chance! Right now, my foot is numb, so I shall just wait here 'til evening."

Of course, we waited there with him, but Lothar, Borab, and I were very anxious about the plan. When Greyl returned, we told her about it and to our surprise found her in enthusiastic approval. It seems that, in her observations of the previous evening, she had felt a gentle strength and true compassion emanating from the Lady, and Greyl had made a quick judgment that the Lady was genuinely Good News!

Greyl also had news about the results of last night's invasion of the town by howling, roaring Demons. The townspeople were clustered in bunches, gesturing and talking about what was experienced by each in the 'raid on the town'. The culmination of the atrocity was the destruction of a grain shed by at least one of the demons, leaving the wood walls in shreds and pieces—and making off with the snares that the farmer had put around the area to protect his fodder! There was a monstrous tooth and several great claws left at the scene. Even from a distance, Greyl had seen these horrendous weapons being passed around and vividly discussed. Greyl practically laughed herself out of the sky over the scenes, and had hurried back to tell us about the demons and savage beasts that now roamed the countryside!

We all looked at one another in wondrous amazement. Even Dromed shook his head in awe, now that his foot was numb and his discomfort somewhat reduced. He said:

"But I am only a gentle old camel...how would they react if they knew?"

I laughed and replied, "Sorry, my gentle old friend, but you are now part of the demonic mob. I guess we shall all have to be a bit more careful wandering around in a very nervous neighborhood."

Solomon had been taking this all in, especially Greyl's observations. He was wryly amused. "That shed probably belonged to one my Lady's ornery uncles. He won't get over its destruction by the Savage Beasts. I do hope that when Dromed presents his snared foot to my Lady, she doesn't put it all together and realizes that he and the Savage Monsters are one!"

"Oh, my—oh, my!" I mused. "What have we done? What have we done?"

"Oh, my—oh, my," mused Borab, "I wonder if I could get my tusk back?"

(My claws? I'd soon grow new ones!)

We all laughed heartily: crisis or adversity seemed always to bring us laughter and a sense of the funny side to anything. We were a rare company of adventurers—tooth and claw not withstanding!

By evening, Dromed's foot was still numb enough for him to walk more easily up to the gate with Solomon for his evening meal with his Lady. Greyl followed discretely to watch and listen for the encounter. The rest of us went back to the stable to wait for their return. We were, needless to say, very anxious about what might happen—and how Solomon's Lady would react to another 'old animal' to nurse.

We had cleaned up a bit so as not to dirty the straw in the stable. Lothar looked infinitely better, neater. Borab and I had adjusted to the loss of some of our weapons, although Borab kept muttering about regaining his lost tusk to keep it out of the clutches of trophy hunters. None of us even remembered that last night's adventures had really been a not-so-simple quest for nourishment, and I never found out—or thought to ask—if any of us had gotten a thing to eat after all that furor! (Or before!)

The wait seemed endless; so did our worries. All three of us, strong as we were, could do nothing to help or protect our comrade. Everything was in the hands of a human—the last creature I ever thought I should have to trust! How we had changed in our perceptions and in our control of situations.

Greyl got back before dark with the good news that Dromed had won the help of Solomon's Lady. She took him on as she had taken Solomon on in his retirement and infirmities. The affection that Solomon and Dromed shared, although she could not really understand, won the help and heart of the Lady. And somewhere, in the deep recesses of her memory, she had a faint, but dim recollection of having met Dromed before.

Greyl was not surprised at the Lady's compassion. She knew the nurturing power of the female of any form of creature…it was instinctual, Greyl explained. This was one kind and good Lady!

The Lady had gently led Dromed, with Solomon, back to her house to remove the snare and treat Dromed's injured foot. No one seemed to be in any danger, so all was truly well. Oh, yes, Dromed had shared Solomon's dinner.

Greyl after her encouraging report flew off to find some food herself, and then watch for any further developments of our friends. She said she would return in daylight, or whenever there was news.

Again, the three of us went out after dark to forage. This time, hopefully, well away from any danger or confrontations with humans, or their dogs, or their sheds.

We returned at dawn with enough food in us to last a while, and we hadn't disturbed the silence of the night.

The next day we napped, resting from our long Journey, but feeling strangely uneasy, as though we should be on our way 'somewhere'. 'Somewhere' seemed to be here, but there didn't seem to be the resolution I thought there would or should be. Greyl checked in to say that all was well with Solomon and Dromed, and to report that Dromed had his foot in a bucket and was receiving special care from the Lady. All parties seemed quite content.

We weren't, however. I was anxious about someone coming down to the stable and discovering us—or worse, that someone being confronted by a wild Bear, a wild Wolf, and a wild Boar. I didn't believe that any Peaceful Intent posture on our part would be effective on a human, especially any human connected to a village that still was traumatized by the specters of demons and savage beasts!

I suggested that we move our daylight cover to the grove of trees near the water-hole. Lothar, Borab, and I went out cautiously to find or make a cover for the three of us.

We dug out a hiding burrow of sorts that could hold us adequately (if not comfortably) until our missing partners returned. We would forage at night, and hide out during the day. If anyone came down to the stable to put clean straw within—as Solomon had told us—there would not be any foreign creatures to set off the community again.

It seemed a long while that we waited for Solomon and Dromed. Indeed, a human did come down to bring clean straw and, thankfully, left no wiser to our occupancy.

Finally, Greyl flew in to announce that our friends were coming back, all eight of their feet in good working condition!

We all met again in the stable, eager to be together once more and eager to hear all the details of their recent adventures. And to hear, finally, the conclusion to Solomon's story that had stopped so abruptly days ago.

Solomon looked especially refreshed and happy.

Dromed proudly showed off his forefoot, working again, and neatly wrapped. His face, radiant, too, bore that as the mark of the Lady's love.

CHAPTER 9

DROMED AND THE KING'S MARK

It was Dromed's story to tell, and with Solomon's affection and encouragement, he related the events of the last evening after the two of them left us:

Dromed said that any anxiety of going up to meet Solomon's Lady and asking for her help disappeared when she appeared there in front of him—and their eyes met for the second time in their lives (the first, so many long years before). He felt those years slip away, and he was young, strong, and handsome again, and she was lithe, radiant, and beautiful. But then, that is exactly what she was, still—tall and elegant in her posture, glowing of countenance, and hand outstretched in loving welcome to him and Solomon. He felt dizzy, and his heart leaped.

Dromed, like Solomon long years before, fell in love! The sad time of being parted from his beloved King evaporated, and his King was replaced by a lovely Queen. He knew that everything would be all right; he would never be safer than now.

He placed his nose in the Lady's hand, and at her touch, all his fears and years of loneliness vanished.

The Lady had put the feed pail down, and Solomon began to eat; but Dromed just stood there and gazed and gazed at her—refreshment of a different kind suffused him. It wasn't until Solomon pulled back, and his Lady guided Dromed's nose into the pail, that he even thought of food—and how good it tasted.

While his face was in the pail, the Lady had looked at his swollen forefoot and the trailing-line.

He heard her exclaim and felt her touch. He flinched ever so slightly but finished off the food before raising his head. This time he lowered his eyes, as tears were in them. He heard her commenting on his condition and understood that she would have to take him up to the house to get 'something' to release the line. He felt both grateful and embarrassed.

She picked up the pail, clucked to Solomon, and placed her other hand under Dromed's head. The three of them went slowly up the hill to her house, her hand supporting and leading Dromed, as if he were wearing a halter. It really wasn't necessary. Dromed, like Solomon, would have followed her anywhere!

She led them to a trough, scooped up some water in her pail, and asked Dromed to put his injured foot in the pail while she went in search of the 'something'.

Dromed meekly obliged and stood waiting, foot in bucket, for the Lady's return. He asked Solomon if he could communicate with this loving human? Solomon replied that he understood her quite well, but she could not understand him except through postures and body-language. When they *first* met, she had seemed to understand that his name was Solomon, when he had said it over and over again to her.

Dromed wondered if he could do the same thing and communicate his name to her. Solomon suggested that they both say Dromed's name to her; she was very intuitive, maybe they would get through!

The Lady returned and felt around for the slide-knot on the snare while his foot was still in the pail. Then, she gently lifted his foot out and tried to release it. It was, of course, deeply imbedded in his ankle, and though soaking in cold water had numbed him slightly, the process hurt immensely. He dared not make a sound: Royal Camels were brave and stoic…(well, rather…but he hadn't been very Royal for years.)

While he was thinking royal and brave thoughts, the line parted in a sudden snap…and he was free!

"Oh, thank God," exclaimed the Lady, "Now let's clean up that injury and wrap it for the night. My, my…what a brave and stoic camel you are, and what is your name, my Royal Camel? I seem to remember you from long ago."

Dromed and Solomon practically shouted: "Dromed…the name is Dromed…please! Dromed!"

"Yes, yes," she said, almost dreamily, "I saw you through an open door, so long ago. You were a pure white camel, a King's mount then, and our eyes met briefly. I felt your concern and your interest...and then you and your Kings were gone, but never forgotten!" She paused, as if in deep thought, then said, "Dromed? Is your name Dromed?"

Dromed and Solomon nodded as vigorously as they could to make the point. The Lady continued, "You met my Solomon the night your Kings were visiting us in the house."

Yes, yes, they nodded, and they both nuzzled her lovingly.

"So, now, we three...from another time...are reunited in the most unforeseen, almost miraculous manner, many many years later. What a special thing it is, to reconnect with that most special of times!" The Lady added, "It means more to me than I can really say!"

Foot washed and wrapped, Dromed with Solomon was led into Solomon's old stall for the night. Their Lady brought them more food, and with gentle caresses bid them goodnight and departed.

Dromed said to Solomon: "Our Lady is so graceful and beautiful, and I am, now, so old and scruffy, I feel completely undeserving of such loving attention!"

Solomon replied, "Haven't you noticed that to her, in her most beautiful self and soul, she sees everything in the light of her special love? And that makes everything and everyone beautiful and lovable? Even shabby old animals like us."

Dromed shook his head, "How can that be? You say her husband is dead. Where is her son, the little Prince? He must be long grown up. Is she all alone? And yet she is full of contentment, love, and joy?"

"Yes," said Solomon, "And I shall complete my story later. It is full of joy and heartbreak, and miracles, too. Rest now my brother, and mend well."

Dromed settled into a deep sleep, still aware of the scent of flowers and the freshness of spring that he had noticed whenever the Lady came near (this fragrance, this aura, in the middle of winter?). As Solomon said, there were miracles present, here. Maybe he and Solomon were part of them!

Dromed and Solomon awakened the next morning to a breakfast of apples, figs—and, most wondrously to Dromed, dates! (He ate the latter, pits and all; it would be crude and rude to spit the pits in front of the Lady, wouldn't it?)

While they were enjoying breakfast, the Lady was unwrapping Dromed's ankle. She remarked that it seemed to be well on the mend, but she had him soak his foot for a while in some herb and plant juice. Dromed was happy to oblige. He loved her attentions.

After the morning soak, the Lady asked Dromed to come outside into bright daylight so that she could address his matted and unkempt coat. Solomon clucked in amusement: "You're in for it now, my friend," he chuckled. "Our Lady is a strict coat-groomer!"

Dromed groaned, not because he disliked the Lady's attentions, but because he really was embarrassed by his scruffy condition. He had been living wild and without care for years. Oh, how he wished he were that handsome, well-groomed, white Royal Camel of old, when he wore the King's livery and walked to bells!

The Lady curried and brushed and tugged and untangled with determination and skill that her elegance belied. Solomon was enjoying the show; Dromed wasn't, but he endured it. He even was washed and scrubbed.

Towards the end of the ordeal, when she was addressing his short, curly mane, she gave an exclamation of surprise. "My goodness," she said, "There is a mark—a brand. Here, on your neck, Dromed. I'll bet you didn't know or remember…you couldn't even bend around to see it."

Dromed didn't remember until that moment. Of course, all his King's royal mounts wore the King's mark. And of course, he could not see his own.

The Lady left them very suddenly and hurried inside her house. She returned immediately, and in her hand, she held a small box—a small gold box, exquisitely embossed and detailed—that she presented to the attention of Dromed and Solomon. On the top was the exact same signature mark which Dromed wore: the King's mark, the Royal Cipher.

Dim, misty memories surfaced. Then, Dromed saw clearly. He remembered the mark from seeing it in his royal days on his livery and on the other mounts. He hadn't remembered that, he, too, bore it.

The Royal Cipher, the Royal Box, the Royal Camel…Dromed felt chills and shakes from the memories that filled him: an open door, a light-suffused room with golden treasures, that beautiful golden box laid at the feet of a beautiful young woman with a tiny child in her arms.

Time stood still, and Time circled around—and they, all three, were young again, just beginning their respective journeys that led them to this time, in this place, in this moment.

Book V

What Is Past Is Only the Beginning

Chapter 1

To Everything a Season—and a Story

Dromed's foot recovered faster than his coat, which the Lady worked over and over daily. He finally looked at her with pleading eyes, and she got the message.

"Dromed, my pet, the years have taken a toll on all of us. Your coat is about as good as I can make it. I shall stop fussing over it. But I wonder if you could do me one small favor?"

Good heavens, thought Dromed, who would have done anything, including giving his life for the Lady. He had tried to communicate his devotion to her: to serve her any way he could.

As Solomon had told him, (and the others) she often chatted amiably to her animals, as with old friends, presuming that they understood. Which, of course, they did.

The Lady continued, "I will never know the full story of how you came here to us—or why—or even with whom. I have long since learned not to question mysteries or miracles. Oh, yes, I know you were not alone: for the damage to Uncle's shed could never have been done by a gentle old camel. I know of no camel with a curved tusk, or claws like scimitars. I shall not reveal that it was you who was caught in Uncle's snare (although I'd love to hang it on his back gate-post and give him some more to worry about!).

"You are Solomon's friend, and mine, too. A treasured link to a very special event. But, as you notice, Solomon is growing blind, more and more so each day, and although I don't like to admit it (especially in front of him) I feel isolated in his blindness. Would you stay here with him—and with me—and be our companion to help Solomon in his infirmities?"

Then the Lady offered Dromed a halter with (joy of joy) camel bells! Now, Solomon would always know where his friend was and the Lady also!

Dromed was overcome with gratitude. Once more, he would walk with bells. He could pretend he was a Royal Camel again and pay homage to a special Queen: his Lady.

The Lady continued: "You will share a pleasant life here with Solomon, and I would be honored to share my life with a Royal Camel, so far from home!"

Dromed almost broke into tears. All he could do was to lean his head gently on the Lady's breast and softly whiffle his acceptance. She understood most adequately, smiled, and stroked his mane.

So, a kind of covenant was established with Solomon, Dromed, and their Lady…and one part of the Journey of the Star was complete.

* * * *

That evening, after their dinner, Solomon and Dromed returned to the stable in the grove to join their friends, and to recount, their most recent adventures.

Lothar, Borab, Greyl, and I were very impressed by Dromed's story, especially when Dromed and Solomon stood together in partnership to share their remaining lives with their Lady. Yet, if truth be told, I think we all were a bit jealous of such a wonderful ending for any animal, and wondered how our Journey of the Star into the Great Unknown would really end for the four of us?

Now was the most appropriate time for Solomon to complete his story. We knew the outcome in the here and now: we were living it, but what about the in-between? Again, I felt that Solomon and his story somehow held the key to our Journey.

Solomon began his story from the point where it left off days and days ago—in reality—years and years ago:

* * * *

Later that night when Solomon's Lady birthed her little son—when all the excitement and all the visitors had disappeared—Solomon walked to the entrance of the stable-cave. Now, early in the morning, the sky was still dark, except for myriad stars, and some particularly brilliant ones right overhead. Solomon sensed distant songs—and bells—and a sort of chiming that seemed to sprinkle the night air and the countryside with stardust, or was it just morning frost?

Solomon drank in the wonder of the whole universe and rejoiced in the life that it bore. He turned to reenter the stable, to take up his position of protection over the sleeping Lady, her newborn, and her Husband. They all must be exhausted, thought Solomon; I am, yet, I am also refreshed and full of some kind of glow (certainly more than that of one lantern).

Oh, it had been a night of miracles, of wonders, of mysteries, and that was more than a little donkey could or should attempt to comprehend. It would be rather hard to get up the next day—after a miracle—and go on with life as usual.

But that is pretty much what they did. As soon as his Lady could travel, the Husband packed up Solomon and himself, carefully lifted up the Lady and the little one onto Solomon, and they went out in search of a better place to stay for a few days before starting for home again. At the same time, the Husband was searching for the registration place in the little town. This official counting requirement was why the Husband and the Lady had had to make their tortuous journey at this time and to this town—in the first place.

Luckily, they found both at the same location. When the Husband registered, a man waiting in the same line offered a room in his house to the Husband, as he (the man) was going to be out of town for about a week.

It really worked out to be another miracle. At this little house, Dromed and his Kings found the family. They heaped and presented gifts to them and stayed only too briefly.

Solomon, having been put up in a small animal shed, never actually saw the Kings. He did, however, meet the Kings' camels and heard all about their trip—and their mission—and their Star Journey. All these details added to the mysteries and miracles. Sometime later, Solomon did see some of the extraordinary gifts that the Kings brought. In fact, it was thanks to the gold that they brought that the Husband could afford a few of the other comforts that the family needed for their journey.

The shed that Solomon was placed in was a huge step down from sharing quarters with his family. It was made exceptionally unpleasant by its existing residents: a cow that never spoke and a rooster that never stopped speaking.

After the camels left—and all the excitement seemed to be replaced with only a noisy exile—Solomon suffered a kind of a letdown which was compounded by the entrance of another donkey onto the scene.

The Husband brought a new donkey into the shed. As gently as he could, the Husband explained to Solomon that they needed another donkey, because plans had been changed; they were not going home, but were going south to Egypt for a while.

Solomon, his head already aching from too much rooster, now felt dizzy from too much happening again, all at once. Well, whatever or wherever Egypt was, it had to be better than this place, he concluded.

"Solomon, this is Samson…Samson, this is Solomon," and the Husband left to get ready for Egypt.

Solomon and Samson eyed each other for a time. Solomon noted that the new donkey was much larger than himself and was obviously a man's mount. That was a relief; he couldn't bear being deposed from being his Lady's donkey. He decided not to make initial conversation. Although, it would be rude not to, it was almost impossible, thanks to the rooster.

Solomon backed out of the shed, dislodging the bar across the door, and walked as far away as he could from the noise. It was a small courtyard, but in its far corner, he could get some relief. He stood in the corner, leaning against the wall.

Samson followed him out and said, "If I weren't partial to hay, I'd eat that bird!"

Suddenly, Solomon decided that maybe Samson wasn't half bad, and maybe they could be friends. He leaned over and touched Samson politely on the nose. "Welcome," he said, "But that bird is too stringy to swallow. Let's go back and *out crow* him!"

Together, they gave the rooster a blast of donkey-honks that even startled the cow. Every time the rooster tried to crow, he got out-honked. He gave up and said meekly, "I was only trying to proclaim what a great day it is and how happy I am"…

"So are we," said Solomon and Samson. And a partnership was born and, for the moment, a blessed silence was won.

The next morning, things were moved out of the house into the courtyard in obvious preparation for the trip. The Lady and her son looked wonderful.

Solomon, although having had the first quiet night in a long while, had spent a sleepless one. He kept seeing the rooster dejectedly sitting on the top of the hay manger, in a posture that all too vividly depicted a crest-fallen fowl, uttering pathetic little clucks deep in his throat.

"I'm sorry," whispered Solomon, "I just meant to limit your loud enthusiasm to more bearable levels and times, like dawn. We're leaving now, so the place is yours—and it is a great day—and we all should be happy!"

As they left the courtyard, Solomon heard the rooster sound off again—loud and clear!

So, Solomon's family—with the Husband on Samson—and the Lady and her son on Solomon (as it should be) set off to the south and the land of Egypt, as had been ordered in a dream. Solomon overheard the conversation about the dream. As his family was very devout and religious, dreams and announcements in them were taken very seriously. Egypt, not home, was their destination, at least for a while.

For Solomon, Egypt was time divided into three parts: a long, sometimes arduous journey; a place away from home that never felt like home; and a long sometimes arduous journey back to real home.

Most of these parts were made more pleasant (almost comfortable) by the Kings' gold, which bought lodging and food and new woolen robes. The stay in Egypt was in an adequate one-room house from which the Husband went out to practice his trade of woodworking. His Lady happily got acquainted with raising her infant son, under the watchful eye of Solomon (when the Husband and Samson were working). When Samson returned, the two donkeys got acquainted and had each other as company. It wasn't too bad a life, but Solomon was homesick, although he very much enjoyed his foster parenthood with, as he called him, 'Young Master'. Of course, he loved every moment that he was with his Lady, although he knew he had to give way to a *human* first-born.

Finally, the time came when in another dream a message told the family that it was safe to return to their real home—and they did…(An arduous journey and then some!)

By now, Solomon's Lady no longer carried an infant cradled in a wrap under her cloak. Young Master was sitting astride Solomon, in front of the Lady. He wasn't very big or heavy yet, and he had just begun walking with the assistance of Solomon's tail—a scene that delighted the Lady and the Husband. Solomon was very aware that young Master considered him *his* donkey. Solomon was pulled and pushed, tweaked and mauled, and in every way tortured by an active young human—and both of them loved every moment! In the ever-mysterious way of childhood, donkey and boy communicated easily with one another. This lasted until human language took over with the boy growing into his species, but the two never quite lost a very loving bond, like that of his mother and Solomon.

So Egypt wasn't all that bad…but arriving home was all that GOOD!

Chapter 2

A Time to Be Young

Even with having been gone several years, home looked to Solomon very much as he had left it. Relatives and friends had taken good care of the house and courtyard. From the Husband's and the Lady's point of view though, much had to be done to restore the house to their requirements. Solomon, however, walked right into his old stall, nosed aside some collected clutter and made himself at home. Samson fit in comfortably, too.

The Lady was young, strong, and very happy to start raising Young Master in his own hometown and environment. The husband was still strong and able to return to his woodworking. Between the two of them, plus helpful relatives and neighbors, home became home again very quickly.

The next ten years or so quickly passed, happily. The Husband employed Samson as his mount and carrier. The Lady and Young Master vied over custodial rights to Solomon—to both he doubled as carrier and playmate.

The Lady, because of her youth and great vitality, had as much fun as a playmate to her son as did Solomon. The three of them would kick around a leather-covered round ball in a kind of run-around game of 'dodge'm', much to the amusement of the Husband who would watch from his workshop. (Solomon usually lost—he was a very big target.)

This was tricky stuff for Solomon, because he had to learn to kick his front feet forward instead of backwards, which to a donkey was the natural motion.

Young Master had his mother's litheness and vigor and, even at a young age, could vault onto Solomon's back—which added to the creativeness of the ball game. He also had imagination and keen intelligence which kept the Lady and Solomon really hopping. Samson who, when not working, was an avid spectator, said to Solomon that Young Master was really taking advantage of him. Solomon was indulging and spoiling Young Master more than his parents.

Solomon replied that being a frisky young colt was over all too quickly, and Young Master would not be this free and active for much longer. He was destined for serious and difficult responsibilities. Solomon knew their days of play and laughter were limited, so he indulged the boy and treasured every moment that they all had together. Their lives would change all too soon.

One particular incident was a memory-maker: the Husband was out on business with Samson; the Lady was doing domestic things in the house, before the afternoon's usual bevy of relatives and friends came to visit. Today, however none appeared; all was quiet.

Solomon and Young Master were building castles and walls of leftover sticks from the woodworking shop. That is, Young Master was building and Solomon was blowing the structures down. As fast as a castle and wall went up, one donkey-snort would bring them down, scattering the sticks.

Frustration led to much laughter but also much determination; and Young Master, ingenious in problem-solving, found a better way of increasing stability with every collapse.

Finally, he decided that the end (up-castle) justified the means (a negotiated non-snort truce). Young Master promised Solomon an equal part in the finale, if Solomon let the finished structure stand for the drama that Young Master had in mind.

Solomon stood back and watched while his boy brought out a small, old sheep-horn and popped a helmet-like pot on his head (boy's head not Solomon's).

The Husband had just returned and Young Master had planned a special surprise to delight his family. The Husband called to his Lady to come out. With the audience in place, Young Master got aboard Solomon, and the rider and mount began to walk around the castle walls, slowly at first, then at a trot, then at a canter.

Young Master pulled Solomon to a dramatic sliding halt, put the sheep-horn to his lips and blew! The tiniest, merest of squeaks came out! Young Master blew again…threeeep! Still, Young Master produced only squeaks (and an increasingly red face).

Oops! Thought Solomon, is this where I come in? He turned his head to question his rider. But Young Master's expression was somewhere between embarrassment and anger, with 'determination' in between. Again. Only squeaks!

I guess it is NOW! Solomon concluded—and he gave a honk that probably was heard all over town! The Husband and the Lady jumped, as did Young Master, and the walls, the castle, everything came down in a pile of dust and sticks!

The two adults almost collapsed in laughter—and cheered and clapped.

"Well," announced the Lady, "That solves the mystery of where my cooking pot went!"

The Husband added, "I really want to be around for the scene when they do Jonah…or Daniel!" (Not me! thought Solomon.)

Well, Solomon concluded, acting-out to tell a story is mighty powerful communication! (The entire cast was rewarded with an apple—which they both shared!)

* * * *

Young Master grew older and started playing with other children his age. He left his mother more and more. There were far fewer times for playing with Solomon. (Actually, the donkey was still an attraction because no one else had a donkey that could do as much as Solomon could—and was treated like a pet.)

Solomon could play ball; Solomon could break up fights (by intruding his furry bulk between adversaries). Solomon could carry as many as five or six riders on him at once—and Solomon could and would sit down and shuck off more riders than were comfortable to him. Solomon was definitely one of the group!

For Solomon, it was absolutely the best of all possible worlds. Young Master was always sensitive and gentle to his four-legged brother and insisted on kindness and respect for all animals wherever he went. Indeed, Young Master was a champion of all life, and that included all ages and sexes (rather unusual for his age and time.)

It wasn't long, though, before Young Master went off to study, sometimes in a school with other boys, sometimes with special tutors. Solomon might take him to a place of learning, but could not do much other than wait patiently at the door for his Young Master to finish his lessons and come out.

Solomon listened to school discussions, but he found them too far over his understanding level. The ideas and the unending list of forefathers' names were boring (too many 'begats'). They were not nearly as interesting as playing games. (But then, humans often were far too wordy.)

Then, it seemed, suddenly, the play times with Young Master were over. After a dozen or so very happy years, Young Master was more engaged in his studies and the Husband's woodworking business than in play. So, Solomon went back to his first love—his Lady—and hung around with his head in her kitchen while she worked and visited with him, as she always had done. Solomon thought of himself as her confidante and friend when no one else was around. They had the first and the most constant bond.

Solomon and Samson were employed to carry around wood before and after it was worked in the shop. Of course, Young Master was involved with the delivery of goods, and Solomon and he never ever lost their bond, although circumstances would find them more and more apart. Wasn't that the trouble with growing up? It usually meant growing apart—though hopefully, only in space, not in affection.

CHAPTER 3

A TIME TO PUT AWAY CHILDISH THINGS

Young Master grew tall and graceful, like his mother. He had to ride Samson now, because on Solomon his feet almost reached the ground. For a time, Solomon thought that he was shrinking with age, but finally admitted that his little boy had grown into a young man, and more and more into the human world.

Every year since the family had returned home from Egypt, they made a special journey to the big city for some sort of religious occasion. They packed up Solomon and Samson. With the Lady on Solomon and the Husband and Young Master taking turns on Samson, they would make the three-day journey to the capital city. This year was to end quite differently from the two dozen or so journeys before.

The donkeys always had enjoyed the change in routine—Samson because he dreamed of adventure and Solomon because he treasured every moment that he could be with his Lady. It was a social occasion also, as there were many other donkeys around in the city and much to see, hear, and smell.

What the humans did, Solomon could only guess, but with the kind of humans that he belonged to, all social activities or religious meetings had to do with a lot of talking and eating—or talking and not eating.

This tribe of humans would rather talk (or argue) than anything! And it did not surprise Solomon that his Young Master was, seemingly, destined to be a wise-talker in his coming days.

Solomon had understood for many years that when the time came for Young Master to go out on his 'mission', he would not be riding on a horse or camel or donkey, but he would be on a special 'service' in the name of Love and Peace.

Oh! thought Solomon. It all makes sense now.

Long years ago, he had wondered why a newborn was called a Prince of Peace. Now, he knew. (But still it seemed to be a very heavy mantle to put on any young man! And, of course, so it turned out!)

It was on the return trip from the capital city this time, that a tragedy befell the family that would forever change their lives—human and animal.

They had just turned into the courtyard of their home. His Lady was riding on Solomon, the Husband was on Samson, and Young Master was walking between, a hand on each donkey as they halted near the house.

Everyone was fittingly tired from a long day's journey, but they had many interesting things to talk about from their visit to the big city. So the conversation among the three humans had made the trip go easier, as they enjoyed each other's observations and opinions.

His Lady had just said that no matter how exciting a trip away from home might be, it was always so very good to be home! The Husband had replied that he agreed heartily, but to him, home was always wherever his Lady was!

Young Master had stopped the donkeys and had turned to smile at them. The Husband dismounted from Samson and held up his arms to assist the Lady. Then, suddenly, he fell down; he just collapsed, falling against Solomon.

Young Master sprang to catch his mother who had lost her balance. They both ended up on the ground almost on top of the Husband. But he was beyond moving or feeling.

He was dead, cradled in his wife's arms—and both of them in Young Master's. Solomon had staggered sideways, and now stood in shock at the scene about him. Samson began to cry in donkey-brays of uncontrolled grief. Both animals had recognized that the Husband was dead before either of the humans understood the reality.

It was an unreal moment in time, accented by Samson's cries and those of the Lady. Young Master, tears streaming down his face, ran out into the street, crying for help. Fortunately, there were people around who heard him and gave their own cries for assistance, as they ran back into the courtyard behind Young Master.

From there on, amidst human cries, confusion took over. Someone seized the halters of both Solomon and Samson and hurried them down to the lower end of the courtyard. Young Master and the Lady—and the Husband's body—disappeared into the house, lost in a grieving community.

The two donkeys, now separated from their human friends, stood close together, trembling in shock and misery throughout the night and the following day. Finally, a kindly neighbor took off their loads of gear and led them to water and feed at the other end of the courtyard. They were not put in their stall because Samson was still sobbing and the noise was almost too much.

Solomon stood by Samson, his head over Samson's neck, all the while trying to soothe his partner. But his own grief just dried up his own sounds as intensely as Samson's grief flooded his!

Solomon had no clear memory of what happened in the following days. Ritual and religious routines occupied the humans, but there was no one who paid attention to the donkeys—and, it seemed no one gave them a thought.

Solomon thought it might have been some days later—after most of the friends and relatives departed, and after all the rituals were over—that Young Master came down to Solomon and Samson. He put his arms around their necks and wordlessly hugged them.

Samson, by this time, had grown hoarse and stopped sobbing. Solomon, head down, just stood motionless, recalling the long and happy years of the past.

Young Master—now, in all appearances a very mature young man—finally spoke, and the bond of boy and animals reconnected. He told them of what a faithful, devoted, and just man the Husband had been. His honesty and fine woodworking, his courtliness and kindness would not be forgotten; and although Young Master's mother was still in shock and deep grief, her heart was full of good memories and trust in her faith. Her grace and strength would carry them all through this dark time.

Then Young Master told them that his cousins and he would continue the wood shop—and would need the help, as before, of the two donkeys to carry things.

He also told them that soon he would be going off in his 'service'—and would often be gone for long times. He said that he counted on his friends to watch over and care for his mother. Then, he addressed Solomon, "Especially you, Solomon, mother's first pet."

To comfort Solomon, Young Master whispered into Solomon's ear the memories of long ago. Near-forgotten secrets and treasures that he and Solomon had shared for many of his growing-up years. The games and jokes and imaginative stories that the two had acted out.

These were priceless—and very personal—memories that Young Master shared again with Solomon. As it turned out, this was the last time that Solomon's boy (now a man) was to have to recount and relive his treasured family life.

Solomon and Samson returned to their stall. Life resumed, almost as they once had known it. Young Master and his cousins took over the wood shop. Lady found time to visit (head-to-head) with Solomon again. Yet, things were very different.

His Lady confided things to Solomon that were personal treasures from the family's past. She also told Solomon of her portent that her son was no 'ordinary man'. He had a destiny that was to lead him into great, revolutionary concepts and also into…but, she never concluded her sentence.

Solomon was greatly puzzled by what she said, not fully understanding what was implied. Later, he was to recollect her words. He understood that his Lady had faith that she would prevail—but her unfinished sentence suggested that her son would not! (At least, in this world.)

It was a shadow that his Lady and Solomon learned to live with. But even with shadows, the sun could and did shine through.

The years went by. Solomon and Samson helped with carrying wood, although both of them were becoming very aged. One day, Samson collapsed in the courtyard, just after carrying in a load of new wood.

Solomon was beside him—both of them in almost the same places that they had been some years before when the Husband dropped dead.

Samson just fell over, his eyes meeting Solomon's in affection and understanding. Then he was dead—and another page of the Book of Life was closed.

Young Master was there and he led Solomon away to his stall, where his Lady took his head between her hands and comforted him. Solomon cried; Lady cried, and Young Master (after he did what he had to do with Samson) cried also, and comforted them both.

Another young, strong donkey was purchased to help with the shop deliveries. Solomon, however, never bonded very much with him. Solomon was used very little now, and only for the exclusive use of his Lady. He spent a lot of time in his stall, dozing and dreaming. Often, Young Master went off on his 'service'. He walked wherever he went, and huge crowds of people followed him.

There were only a few times that Solomon carried his Lady to see and hear her son. All that the donkey could get from the occasions was an atmosphere of excitement and enthusiasm, mixed at times, with a presence of Peace in the midst of chaos. Solomon wondered if his little boy—his Prince of Peace—would ever—or could ever—dwell in any Peace himself, when such powerful emotions seemed to surge around him and in all his followers, and, yes, his enemies. (There were those.)

But he knew his boy—and that boy could bring Peace if it was called for—and faith and hope too. As for Love, Solomon knew all about that! Or, he thought he did!

CHAPTER 4

THE GREATER LOVE

"Solomon," I cried, "Don't stop now; don't leave us hanging again!"

Solomon had stopped talking. He had left us once again, without resolution to his story.

Dromed leaned over and nudged Solomon with his nose, but his friend had that misty, faraway look in his eyes, once more, that signified that he was somewhere else, deep in his memories.

Lothar, Greyl, Borab, and I exchanged frustrated murmurs and glances.

Dromed said softly, "From what Solomon has hinted, I expect that he finds it far too hard to go on with his story. Maybe later, old friend?"

Solomon nodded vaguely, and the rest of us moved restlessly, wondering how to handle our present situation. We wanted—and didn't want—a resolution. Solomon paused for what seemed endless time and then said, abruptly and without preface: "They killed him…they put him to death!"

"Who?" we all said in unison, "Who killed whom?"

"They," replied Solomon, "they killed Young Master!"

"Why? And who are they?" I anguished.

Solomon replied, "Young Master was too dangerous, too…what humans say, too revolutionary. He was a threat to someone's territory or power or something. I don't understand any of it—a donkey is on the lowest level of civilization. How can I (of all creatures) understand power?

"I just know that he was put to death for whatever he taught the huge crowds that loved him. He taught Peace, he taught Love...and he was killed by those who hated and feared him! That's all!"

"That doesn't make sense," said Dromed. "How can anyone kill Love...or Peace, for that matter? These are ideas, climates to live in!"

It was clear that none of us, wild or domestic, could understand such an ending to such a story as Solomon's...I guess it was a case of destroying the message-bearer.

Solomon, then, went on to say that this had all happened less than a year ago, in the big city, at a time of a great religious occasion. He had never been given a complete report of the real happenings. He had not taken his Lady to the city that time; he was too old and too infirm...and for once, he was thankful to have been left out...and not know the full details.

Lady had been brought home by family and friends, and they had stayed for a time to counsel and comfort one another. Some of them were still here.

Lady, herself, although bearing a very special and personal grief, seemed to have drawn on a very special and personal grace. Her beautiful self and soul were even more peace-filled and loving...and she seemed to live in an aura of unusual joy and radiance, never fully understood by others.

Solomon told us all this with tear-filled eyes, but he, too, had drawn much comfort from the Lady's strength, and he did not question, really, the 'whys' or 'who's' as we had done. He treasured his memories and the humans that made them happen. That was enough for one little (now old) donkey. It was all about a Greater Love, anyway, and that *he* believed *anyone* could understand.

And us? Was this all enough for us? Was this remarkable story (indeed, all our remarkable stories) the end of our (my) Journey of the Star into the Great Unknown? Had we all come together, over such distances and seasons to find our goal in one little, old donkey? And in a human story perceived by a little, old donkey? But was it just a human story?

* * * *

There was then a very long time of silence among us. None of us moved; none spoke. Time seemed to go on forever without us.

Lothar finally said thoughtfully, "I remember a time when you and I, Zar, were hostile and fearful of all humans. We couldn't see how anything good could come from them! Now we see a lot of good in their society, as well as a lot of bad, such as greed or selfish power that kills off the good."

He continued, "Will we, as animals, ever be able to reach across our differences and share, say, Peaceful Intent or a climate of Peace, or even a bridge of Love?"

Greyl replied, "We already have. We couldn't be more different from one another, yet we have set aside differences to help each other in friendship. Fur, feathers, or flesh, can't we all understand Love?"

"Food for thought," I added, always trying to sort out ideas. Again, there was a long silence.

Borab was the one to break it. He mumbled, "If *thought* were *food*, what am I doing here? Working so hard for you all!" He clicked his tusks.

Startled by such an abrupt change of mood and its incongruity, we all laughed, refreshed as ever by the way we always could find healing humor in even our most difficult times. (Borab usually grounded us!)

Dromed said, "As outrageous as you make yourself out to be, Borab, I remember all too well that you did not hesitate to put those precious tusks of yours into the snare around my foot to free me! You're just a big act!"

"Nonsense," said Borab, "I'm just always eager to taste new things!" (click, click)

Outrageous, indeed, I thought. Here we are, absolutely stunned by an altogether differently 'outrageous' act, and we are joking around like Dromed's Royal Fools, as he called us, long ago, in his oasis, when we met.

And yet as always, we had to lighten the load of the moment. A laugh among friends, especially with us, was a renewal of 'love', a bond among friends. I just hoped Solomon understood.

Solomon, honest, solid, big-hearted, probably understood. I believe he always had understood and now, he was just waiting for us truly to understand: That his story was about Life and fully living it, with all its laughter and sorrow. And also about Love, a love greater even than dying…greater than Death!

Chapter 5

Every Step of a Journey Is the Journey

The sound of bells brought me back to reality. I guess I had drifted off into my own thoughts so deeply that time had seemed to stop. It looked as though my companions, too, had been deep into their thoughts, because the sound of Dromed's halter bells made us all jump.

"Solomon," he said, "it is time to go up to meet our Lady."

The two of them went out, leaving the four of us in the stable to sort out our own exits, or whatever we agreed upon as our next steps.

Indeed, now we had to consider where to go, or what to do. The Star had disappeared. It had seemingly finished with us—or for us…or, maybe it had led us to Solomon and the beginning of his special story, thirty some years too late? Our Journey was ended. Now what?

Borab broke the silence: "I don't know about you, my friends, but I am going out to find food for more than thought. I'm coming for you, my little root delicacies. You can hide, but you can't run!" Off he trotted.

Lothar, for once, said he wasn't hungry.

Greyl said she'd wait for morning.

As for me? I reached up to touch my Star Stone for comfort; it had not left, it was still with me. But, I felt keenly that I was between two worlds, and neither had to do with eating.

Lothar and I looked at one another, questions hanging in the air. Where do we go from here? Without hesitation, in unison, we said, "The Cedar Mountains!"

Of course! The Cedar Mountains, not far away, were the closest place we could go. There, it felt like the homelands of our youth—evergreens, mountains, snow. Of course! We would go 'home.'

Greyl, whose bill was under her wing, but whose bright, beady eyes were on both of us, said: "I know just the place, a haven for two, old, weary, wilderness wanderers like yourselves. You are sticking together, I presume?"

Lothar said, "Wouldn't have it any other way. Zar is my first and oldest friend. Wherever he goes, I go."

I replied earnestly, "Lothar and I, hopefully, will never be parted—where one goes, the other goes!"

As for Greyl? She said she had a plan that involved a nice lake to the east of our present location. And there were other marshy places where geese spent the whole year in abundance of grains. She would check up on her 'boys' anytime she could—and would always keep an eye on our well-being.

Lothar and I knew that Greyl—the faithful—would live up to that commitment. She had literally opened a way for us since early in our Journey. She had scouted for trails, food, and danger.

She had watched over us like a Divine Angel, and I wasn't the only one who wondered if she really was a goose and not a special mothering spirit from the realms of cloud and wind (or a blessing from heaven itself).

What had taken us earthbound creatures a lifetime to travel could have been accomplished by Greyl in less than one moon's cycle. Why had she chosen to spend her lifetime helping earthlings on a star trip to 'whatever' when her sky was full of stars beckoning her to 'everywhere'?

To Lothar and me, words would never be adequate to tell her how much we appreciated her and her help. (For the life of me, I could not figure out how ever to hug a goose and tell her how much I loved her! We would never have finished this Journey without Greyl.)

Then, there was the matter of Borab. He sallied in, at that very moment, with a body wrap of dried mud coated with a thatch of chaff, carrying some chunks of stuff daintily held in his mouth (I think for Borab, words would have to suffice!)

He laid the chunks in front of me and said: "I washed these carefully before I brought them to you. Try them. Honestly, they taste a lot better than they look."

From a distance, Lothar said, "They need to."

I knew that I had to accept Borab's delicacies because he was truly generous and most untypical in his sharing of his food.

Actually the 'whatever's' were very good. "Lothar," I said, "you are missing something here: This is delicious!"

I gave a piece to him. He trusted me enough to try it—or he felt it better not to show bad manners.

"You're right…I apologize, Borab." To make amends Lothar asked if we could go out later and find a few more of Borab's 'whatever's'?

"Anytime, my friends—anytime—plenty more where these come from. Farmers plant these roots, but they never harvest them all, because humans can't smell them, and humans don't understand the underground behavior of these critters. Don't jump, Zar…they're plants not animals. I told you they can hide, but they can't run!"

At that instant, Solomon and Dromed returned looking extremely happy and pleased with themselves. Dromed's wrapping was gone, and he seemed to have a little trouble recalling which foot he should limp on.

He said, "I am so grateful to Solomon's Lady for taking me on. I hope it doesn't stretch her resources too much."

Solomon replied, "Camels are not employed much around here. Donkeys are cheaper and easier to handle. I think when people see such an unusual pet with the Lady, they may all contribute to Dromed's 'date and fig fund'. You can look pitifully needy, can't you, old friend? The limp would definitely help too."

We all laughed, and we all thought it a promising plan. But what was even better was the promise of a comfortable and loving future for our two 'domestic' friends—one who thought himself a special Royal Camel and the other who thought himself one of the lowest of the load-bearers. They were close friends—and always would be.

I wondered if one thought of himself as a lowly, common, baggage-camel, and the other thought of himself as a Royal donkey, would they still be friends? Of course! Our suits, our outside livery (so to speak) or lack of it was as nothing compared to the deeper knowledge—that of knowing and recognizing the love of a friend. No matter our suits: I in a bear suit, Lothar in the fur of a wolf, Greyl in a cloak of feathers, and even old Borab in his suit-of-the-day—be it mud or chaff or boar bristles—we knew we were friends and loved.

Our outer selves were really so unimportant or so transparent, as Solomon so wisely expressed about his Lady, what mattered was the beautiful self and soul that shone though. I guess that could even extend to humans (my, how far I'd come!).

Now, we had to say farewell to our friends to complete our final journeys—wherever they led.

Solomon and Dromed, we were sure of. But, what about Borab?

He said, he'd go with Lothar and me as Greyl led us to the Cedar Mountains. He wanted to see whether that would be a place to 'start off again from' or a place to 'end up at'. (That was Borab, the opportunist!)

For the time being, we made no immediate plans to leave Solomon and Dromed. After all, we were all old and we had just learned the conclusion of Solomon's story. There was no real need to hurry.

Somehow, short of a miracle, we remained out of human sight. We always managed to be out of the shed for the straw-changing. (The idea of a random hayfork hitting a bear or a wolf or a wild boar was horrendous, if not impossible to imagine or explain)!

The nights were used for hunting food (for the wild ones) and the days were spent recounting our many adventures for those of our company who were not involved in the first legs of our Journey.

Borab's favorite story was about Lothar and the fish hunt (under water). Dromed was enthusiastic about the mountain adventures with the goats. Solomon loved the Bear Bellow event (past and present). Greyl's favorite was when the bent-over tree whipped back and sent me tumbling.

All six of us had a wonderful time recounting our varied escapades and, of course, they became better with each retelling. The humorous adventures were always the best. It is always interesting how funny any event can be once it's over and survival (or triumph) is the outcome!

There was not one of us who wasn't old now; the recollections went back into our very strong and youthful days, and we all seemed to take on some of that vitality again. We were an amazing collection of miracles in timing and occasion, over and over again. Leadership had changed with the challenge and even food habits had been altered with need. Perhaps that was the real message: that we had tried the Journey, accommodated to the necessary changes required, and we had made it!

In the end, every one of us recognized the Miracle aspect of the Journey and accepted the Mystery rather than the Meaning of the end and the means.

We were special creatures—Lothar, Greyl, Borab, Solomon, Dromed, and I—all speaking a common language, that of friend and partner. The only downside? The bridge to humans was still to be built in the future. Maybe? Or, was that idea just a dream?

* * * *

And so we finally went on our way—sent off on the richness of love and the bonds of friendship. Secure in the knowledge that Solomon and Dromed had their Lady as their resource; the three of us had the Cedar Mountains for ours; Borab would drop in and out when he desired. And all of us, seemingly, would always have Greyl! Could it get any better than this?

Greyl had scouted out the perfect 'haven' for Lothar and me, she said. The long trip was easy and uneventful, although we did miss following our white camel, as we had the first time.

The Cedar Mountains were just as beautiful and wild as we first thought, and Lothar and I knew that they would be 'home' for us. Borab was happy to use them as his base, also; although he meant to wander, as was his style, while Lothar and I wanted to stay at home—a luxury that we had not thought we wanted until now.

No more Journeys for us, just the glories of sunrises and sunsets and green cedars and views across mountains to an azure sea in the western distance.

That was the view from the cave that Greyl had found for us. It was high on a mountainside, with dramatic outlooks east, west, and south. It was safe and cozy and clean. Lothar and I couldn't believe that it wasn't heaven on earth…maybe it was!

From time to time, Greyl and Borab dropped in to check up on us. Did we have enough to eat? Oh, yes. Were we warm (or cool)? Oh, yes. Were we content? Delightfully so, for a pair of wanderers. Everything was a 'yes' and a 'thank you'. The only sadness was in our missing Dromed and Solomon. But we had wonderful memories; oh, did we have memories!

Chapter 6

The Dream of Althazar

Lothar and I were stretched out full length on the ledge in front of our cave, catching some of the last rays of an early spring sun. We had slept lazily though the end of winter, but had managed to rouse ourselves to search for food and to bask in the sun's warmth whenever the need arose.

The view from our ledge was so magnificent we could seldom ignore it for long. This morning the sunlight had danced fitfully through snow squalls, raising up rainbows in fleeting arches over the sea to the west.

Now, the sea reflected clouds and sunlight as the snow showers headed out over it. The scene was ever-changing and ever-exciting.

Lothar, pedaling his feet in the air, broke the silence. "This must be heaven. I can't think of any place that could improve on our 'home' here, can you?"

I replied, "No, unless this is all just a dream."

"Don't wake me," said Lothar. "Seriously, it can't be a dream because we are in it together, experiencing the same things. What about our Journey, was that, too, a dream? Could six of us act individually and collectively in the same lifelong dream?"

"It doesn't matter," I said. "I really don't care—either way it was a wonderful lifelong adventure."

Lothar, right side up again, persisted: "Throughout this whole life that we've shared, you and I, and all of us, we have had the curiosity—almost a need—to ask questions along the way. Now with age and time to think long thoughts, which do you believe are more important: the questions or the answers?

I did not hesitate in the reply; this was one Idea that I really embraced. "I believe, now, that the *questions* are the most important, those ongoing, eternal, *what ifs*!"

Lothar's ever-expressive eyebrows and ears arched up: "What about the answers, all those long-sought answers that we chased all through the whole Journey? Aren't they the end of all our quests, all our questions, all our dreams?"

"No. 'Ends' are not the real issue in my life anymore," I replied. "I believe that questions are the driving force that keep us 'truly alive' in this world. Answers are ever-changing as we live and change, and…" (I paused to take a deep breath) "…we should always be asking old and new questions. Questions are the fire in the belly."

Lothar paused. Then quizzically asked, "And dreams…what about dreams?"

"Oh, my friend," I mused, "dreams are entirely something else…they are the honey on the tongue."

There was a long and thoughtful pause (at least on my part), as I rolled over the memories of fire and honey. Lothar, ever the active one, had turned to some profound discussions in his old age. Seldom before had he held so still in his actions, as to express himself this way.

Now seemed the right time to bring out the subject which I held so dear—Dreams and Miracles—both of which seemed inextricably entwined.

I continued, "Just think how miraculous it was that none of us were ever injured or even killed in all our adventures. You might have drowned in your crazy fishing ventures. Greyl might have been snared again or been blown into a mountainside in some of those fierce winter blizzards. Dromed might have died of complications from that foot injury. Even I might have been eaten by that huge savage beast!"

"Great heavens," exclaimed Lothar, sitting bold upright, "Zar, you were the Huge Savage Beast!"

"Oh yes…I was, wasn't I?" I, too, sat up, feeling a little foolish.

Lothar tried to make me feel a little less silly, "Hey, my friend…give us a big Bear Bellow, right now. Scare the devil out of this place, just in case something is looking to eat us!"

I let go with one of my finest Bear Bellows! The echoes were still jumping back and forth though the mountains when a flurry of wind and feathers hit our ledge. Lothar and I also jumped!

It was Greyl. "Are you all right?" She said, breathlessly.

"What are *you* doing..." I asked, also breathlessly, "just cruising around over our mountain keeping us under watch?"

"No, no," she replied, "I was just coming in for a visit when the roar hit the mountainside. You *do* get better with age, Zar...you're really powerful, impressive!"

I was glad something got better with age.

Lothar said to Greyl, "I've got to confess something to Zar, and I need a little backup in case he doesn't believe me. It's sort of in line with our talking about Miracles."

"Good heavens, you two," I said, "what awful secret has Lothar kept from me that he needs support in telling his best friend?"

Lothar moved around to face me and his amber eyes met mine in a very serious expression. He dropped his gaze and lowered his head. I thought he was going to roll over and pedal his feet in the air. I couldn't imagine what it could be that had my wolf partner acting like a naughty puppy. Even Greyl looked puzzled; Lothar was always a very open and strongly confident character. (He only put on his silly puppy act to be funny.)

Finally he spoke: "You probably don't know this, Zar, but you have always been the only one of us who ever saw the Star! We all called it our Journey of the Star to the Great Unknown because you invited all of us to come with you on *your* Star Journey—and we made it ours—but not one of us ever *saw* the Star that you followed."

I looked in bewilderment at Lothar and Greyl. I reached to touch my Star Stone. "You never saw the...my Star? But you made a Journey of a lifetime, all of you, on only my story, my vision of my Guiding Star?"

"Lothar is telling you the truth," said Greyl. "None of the other five of our team ever saw what you saw. We just believed in your mission and your vision and your commitment!"

"That's about it," said Lothar, finally meeting my gaze. "We believed in you—and trusted you; we didn't need a Star...we had you!"

I felt overwhelmed and shaky, almost as if I had awakened from a dream that was so very real that when I awakened and found that it was all a dream, I still thought I was living it! I guess until now, I was.

"Does it really matter?" asked Greyl, "We went along with you because you saw a Star and committed your life to following it. And although I often mapped out the trail, you were always using your thinking and your Ideas to move us forward. I think that is especially wonderful. No doubt about it: You are a real thinking bear, Zar.

"We believed in you, just as Dromed and his caravan believed in their Kings' Star, although none of them ever saw it."

Lothar continued, "Solomon, like Dromed, said he only saw a glow or a radiance. He, too, never saw a Guiding Star, but the Kings did—and I think Solomon said the shepherds did. You, Zar, were apparently singled out as one special animal—as there were special humans—to see the Star, and to follow it, then to convince others to follow it on trust (faith?) alone."

Folding her wings contentedly to cradle her body, Greyl gently concluded: "You are part of a Miracle—and so were…are…we. We believed in you! And because of your belief in us as your companions of the Star, we came to believe in ourselves—that's a gift. To have a Star to follow, and to find others to share that vision is the greatest adventure, the greatest Journey in life itself."

It was quite a while before I could speak again. I must admit, it took some serious thinking…and absorbing…of the Ideas put forth…of the Truth of my friends' words.

Finally, I found my own: "It seems that some have to see to believe; others have to believe to see. Either way, the six of us were uniquely blessed by each other's company, by the guidance of our Star and my Star Stone, and most importantly, by the Magnitude and Miracles of the Journey itself."

* * * *

Now, I wondered, how long will it take for another Star to appear—to start someone else on another Journey? And who of God's creatures will lead? And who will follow?

There was a long interval of silence. Time was no longer terribly relevant to our present lives—only food and contentment and, of course, memories took priorities now.

I gave a leisurely yawn. Greyl fluffed a few feathers. Lothar rose up slowly and stretched fore and aft in his elegant wolf way.

He grinned at me. Even with several front teeth missing, it was that sly, wicked grin of old.

"Zar," he said, "let's go over to our special snow-slope and have a refreshing roll and slide. You're not too old or lazy for that, are you, my friend?"

I grinned back: "I bet I can beat you to that slope!"

And, Greyl, from not too far under her wing, was heard to sigh, or maybe, chuckle and say: "I shall wait up for you!"

Epilogue

There have been legends told in the last nineteen or so centuries about some mysterious sounds echoing through the High Lebanons:

On some moon-dark nights, under a canopy of stars that seem to sparkle and dance in the silence of cosmic winds, there is heard an incredible roar of some great beast…it is answered, always, by the haunting howl of a wolf. And, sounding high above is the trumpet call of one, lone goose.

Now, there are, presumably, no lions left near that coast of the Mediterranean Sea…and wolves are few, if at all. Of course, geese are around in flocks at most times.

Yet…

These sounds seem larger and more evocative than the obvious explanations…they seem, always, to be together; and they seem to recall a wild, untamed Song of Celebration for a long-forgotten Journey—or even for an ancient convocation.

Some say that these are the cries of lost souls looking for something (or some place) in the sanctuary of the high mountains…on those dark, lonely nights, could they be searching to call back a Dream?

Or…

Isn't it possible that these are really love songs of some magnificent, bygone creatures who have already found it?

978-0-595-41334-8
0-595-41334-X

Printed in the United States
63983LVS00005B/67-90

9 780595 413348